The Hunt

Overhead, a craft that looked like a silver running shoe tore across the sky. It was followed by something that looked like a flying steam iron with torpedo-shaped outriggers. Both vessels fired energy weapons at something out of sight behind the base houses. Whatever they hit went "Crump!" There was a lot of smoke.

"What on Earth…" Her father turned an incredulous face to Merle. "No. Cancel that. Nothing *on Earth*. Friends of yours?"

Merle shook her head. "Far from it. This is a close encounter of the fourth kind."

Her father stared. "The fourth kind?"

Merle ducked as a horseshoe-shaped craft powered overhead. "Yeah – that's where the aliens shoot at you."

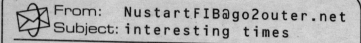

A message to our Earth Friends

Sector Commander Miraz has retired. I am the new commander of Rigel sector. In recognition of the good work being undertaken by Friends agents on Earth, your connection to the Outernet has been upgraded. You can find out more by logging on.

Here are your instructions:

1 – Start reading this book. The first password is the name of Zodiac's ship.

2 – Log on to the Outernet by typing www.go2outer.net into your internet browser – then enter this password to begin your adventure.

When you have done this, enter your agent ID if you are already a Friend, or register as a new Friend with the FIB.

Remember to open all your o-mails, and explore your FIB Files and Links – this is important!

Enjoy your new connection – let's hope it doesn't get taken over by the FOEs!

Keep smart, keep safe.

Commander Nustart
Sector Commander, Rigel Sector
FIB (Friends Intelligence Bureau)

You must maintain the link – visit the website

WWW.GO2OUTER.NET

The Hunt

Steve Barlow and Steve Skidmore

SCHOLASTIC

IMPORTANT

Once you have logged on to the Outernet you will be given important passwords and I.D. numbers – remember to write these down on the special page at the back of this book.

Scholastic Children's Books,
Commonwealth House, 1–19 New Oxford Street,
London WC1A 1NU, UK
a division of Scholastic Ltd
London ~ New York ~ Toronto ~ Sydney ~ Auckland
Mexico City ~ New Delhi ~ Hong Kong

First published by Scholastic Ltd, 2002
Copyright © 2003 by Steve Barlow and Steve Skidmore
in association with The Chicken House Publishing Ltd.
Cover artwork © Matt Eastwood, 2003

Outernet is a trademark of Transcomm plc in various categories
and is used with permission. Outernet and Go2Outernet are also
trademarks in other categories for The Chicken House Publishing Ltd.

ISBN 0 439 98209 X

Printed and bound by Cox and Wyman Ltd, Reading, Berks

2 4 6 8 10 9 7 5 3 1

The right of Steve Barlow and Steve Skidmore to be identified as the
authors of this work has been asserted by them in accordance with the
Copyright, Designs and Patents Act, 1988.

OUTERNET WEB SITE
Created by Big Thumb Studios Inc., La Crescenta, CA 91214, USA
Using original material created by Jason Page, 'Table Top Joe' and Mark Hilton
All copyrights © Steve Skidmore, Steve Barlow and The Chicken House

Friends Intelligence Bureau

FIB ORIENTATION FILE

THIS IS A TOP SECURITY PROTECTED
FILE FOR FRIENDS' EYES ONLY.
THIS INFORMATION MUST NOT BE
COPIED, DUPLICATED OR REVEALED TO
ANY BEING NOT AUTHENTICATED AS A
FRIEND OF THE OUTERNET.

Info Byte 1 – The Outernet. The pan-Galactic Web of
information. Created by The Weaver for the free exchange
of information between all advanced beings in the Galaxy.

Info Byte 2 – The Server. Alien communication device
and teleportation portal. The last such device in the hands
of the Friends of the Outernet.

Info Byte 3 – Friends. Forces who are loyal to The Weaver
in the struggle to free the Outernet from the clutches of
The Tyrant.

Info Byte 4 – FOEs. The Forces of Evil, creatures of The Tyrant who seek to use the Outernet to control and oppress the people of the Galaxy.

Info Byte 5 – Bitz and Googie. Shape-shifting aliens disguised as a dog and a cat respectively. Bitz is a Friends agent (code-named Sirius) and ally of Janus. Googie (code-named Vega) was formerly a FOEs agent, but claims to have defected to the Friends.

Info Byte 6 – Janus. A Friends Agent who, while trying to keep The Server from the FOEs, disappeared into N-Space.

Info Byte 7 – Jack Armstrong. A fourteen-year-old human from England who became wrapped up in the fate of The Server when it was given to him as a birthday present. **Merle Stone and Lothar (Loaf) Gelt.** Jack's American friends from the nearby US Air Force base who have been helping him keep The Server safe from the FOEs.

Info Byte 8 – Tracer. The Tyrant's Chief of Surveillance, who tried to take The Server for his own purposes and is now on the run.

Info Byte 9 – Zodiac Hobo. Space-hippy and self-styled desperado who gave Jack and friends a lift in his spaceship Trigger.

PROLOGUE

Secret Headquarters of The Tyrant,
The Forbidden Sector

Bugs are among the most feared creatures in the Galaxy. Their muscle-bound, thick-skinned grey bodies and serious lack of social responsibility cause high levels of anxiety, stress and agony wherever they appear.

Eyeball-Popping Razor-Toothed Ear-Drillers from the planet Aaaaaargh! are also high on the list of beings most likely to make a life form's tentacles turn to jelly and antennae tie themselves in knots, along with an embarrassing loss of bladder control.

But these creatures are pussycats compared with The Tyrant. The Tyrant is leader of the Forces of Evil and holder of the title *Most Foul, Wicked and Depraved Being in the Galaxy* (as voted for ten Galayears running by all other foul, wicked and depraved beings in the Galaxy, and they should know what they're talking about).

The Big Bug, leader of the Bugs, was standing in total darkness and total fear. It had been summoned to the Dark Pyramid, the secret headquarters and main fortress of The Tyrant. The Big Bug had teleported from the prison planet of Kazamblam, thus avoiding the vast array of defences that protected the Dark Pyramid from any being stupid enough to want to attack the mighty and impregnable construction.

Being summoned before The Tyrant was bad. It was worse than bad – much worse. Many of the Big Bug's predecessors had been summoned there before him. They had never returned; and soon after their visit, their positions had been prominently advertised as an employment opportunity in magazines featuring big guns on the cover and short words inside. This unnerving fact was preying on the Bug's mind as it stood in the darkness.

A blinding light exploded, illuminating the surroundings with the brilliant radiance of a thousand stars.

The startled Bug blinked, trying to take in its surroundings. When it had done so, it whimpered.

It was standing in a huge cavern on the edge of a mighty precipice that disappeared downwards into utter blackness. A thin metal bridge spanned the colossal chasm. It shimmered silvery-blue against the blackness of the drop.

Stepping back, the Bug peered across the abyss. It could just make out the dark outline of a figure silhouetted against the array of lights. The Tyrant took every precaution to conceal his identity, even from his most senior officers.

The Tyrant's voice boomed out, echoing from every wall. "You are standing on the edge of The Bottomless Abyss of Unspeakable Oblivion. Both literally and metaphorically," he added.

Although the bug didn't understand the exact meaning of "literally and metaphorically", the implication was clear enough. Its armpits began to dampen.

"Of course, the abyss isn't *really* bottomless," continued The Tyrant, "although it is awfully deep. If you should fall into it, you would eventually find yourself in an ice-cold sea. Can you swim?"

The Bug shook its huge grey head.

"Not to worry. You wouldn't drown."

The Bug gave a sigh of relief.

"Because the sea is home to thousands of Flesh-Ripping Piranha Squid from the Planet Aaaaaargh! They're the sea-dwelling cousins of the Eyeball-Popping Razor-Toothed Ear-Drillers, by the way, and their existence explains why the Eyeball-Popping Razor-Toothed Ear-Drillers never learned to swim. But perhaps you're not interested in zoology." The Bug began to sweat harder. "Interesting creatures," continued The Tyrant. "In a matter of seconds, they can strip the flesh off a fully grown Nawgaw." The Evil Lord of the FOEs paused pointedly. "Or a Bug…" he added, playfully.

The Bug began to sweat even more.

"What did your mother and father call you?"

A shadow of confusion crossed over the Bug's grey, horned features. What was The Tyrant playing at? The question was ridiculous – Bugs weren't born. They were the result of a genetic experiment, which crossed an

Antarean rhinocerous with a Lalandian hyena.

"Everyone should have a name," continued The Tyrant. "What about Eric? That's a good name. A solid name. A … dependable and reliable name."

"As your Appalling Majesty wishes," replied Eric.

"Good. Now, Eric, this is what we are going to do. You are going to walk across this bridge. I will ask you a question. You will reply. If it is a question to which you can honestly answer 'yes', you may take one step forward. If your answer is negative, you will take two steps back. The object of the exercise is to reach this side of the abyss."

"And if I don't?"

In the silence that followed, the Bug swore it could make out the lapping of water far below it.

"So," the Tyrant began, "Eric. You are leader of the Bugs, chief enforcers of my Forces of Evil?"

"Yes," answered the Big Bug.

"There, wasn't that easy? And that is not a question!" warned The Tyrant before the Bug could answer. "Take one step forward." The Bug complied, stepping out on to the thin metal that separated it from the terrifying drop.

"You are feared throughout the Galaxy?"

"Yes."

Another step.

"There is an unending supply of Bugs."

"Yes."

Another step.

"Therefore you are expendable…"

There was a slight tremor in the Bug's reply. "Er … yes."

"Good. Take another step forward."

A further series of satisfactory answers brought the Bug to the middle of the bridge.

An electronic hum sounded behind the Bug. Startled, the creature turned. The part of the bridge it had walked over had retracted into the shimmering metal wall. The Tyrant's voice was cold and measured. "To help concentrate your mind," he explained.

The Bug gulped. The only way now was forward … or down.

"I seem to recall," said The Tyrant, "that you promised to capture the last remaining Server in Friends hands, so that I might take complete control of the Outernet. Correct?"

"Yes."

The Bug took a step forward, away from the terrifying drop.

"Not only that, you promised to capture The Weaver, the leader of the Friends."

"Yes."

Another step forward. Another step nearer to safety.

"Have you?" The Tyrant spat out the question.

"No," the Bug's voice was almost a whisper.

"Take two steps back."

The Bug did as it was ordered. Its heels hung over the

edge of the thin metal. It stood eyes closed, waiting for the inevitable, final question.

Something began to play a strangulated electronic version of Dr C Rapper's hit single, *Baybee, I Wanna Feel Your Tentacles Round Me All Night Long.* The Tyrant gave an exasperated sigh. "What now? Interruptions, interruptions." The Dark Lord flicked a switch, and waved vaguely at the Bug. "Excuse me a moment while I take this call."

The head of Tracer, the FOEs Chief Surveillance Officer, appeared on a bank of screens on The Tyrant's communications console. The six-armed being's elephant ears drooped in a dispirited sort of way, and his VR visor, usually pulsing with light, was dark and lifeless.

"Tracer, how good of you to get in touch. Where are you? No, don't bother answering." The Tyrant checked a set of coordinates. "I see, a Trading Post in the Trojan Sector."

A bead of sweat broke out on Tracer's brow. He wiped it away with two of his six claws.

"I was just discussing your latest failure with my Head of Security." The Tyrant's voice was as cold as the sea at the bottom of the abyss. "I understand that you travelled to a planet called Helios and took The Server from the three humans, namely Jack Armstrong, Merle Stone and Lothar Gelt – and their renegade chameleoid companions."

"Yes, your Gracious Evilness," replied Tracer.

"Yet you did not return it to me. I wonder why that was?"

Tracer remained silent.

"Perhaps you wanted it for yourself? Perhaps you see yourself as a Dark Lord? Although, since your visor is obviously not functioning, it would appear that you no longer *see* anything."

"It is as you say, Malign Majesty…"

"I have *interviewed* the surviving Bugs who accompanied you to Helios. They informed me (between pleas for mercy) that once you had let The Server slip from your grasping claws and lost track of it – along with the humans and their Friends – you stole an escape pod from their ship and disappeared." The Tyrant paused for effect. "However, you will be delighted to know that The Server has turned up again."

Tracer gave a start.

The Tyrant gave a low chuckle. "I thought that might surprise you."

"Where is it, O Vexatious One?"

The Tyrant ignored the question. "Frankly, I am disappointed in you."

Tracer nodded furiously. "I know, Your Most Deplorable Wickedness. And because of that I wish to tender my resignation."

"The job I gave you was for life. Or in your case, death."

Tracer's thin lips twitched. "I suppose a reference is out of the question?"

"I promise you a very generous severance." The Tyrant's voice sent a chill through both of Tracer's complex spines. "I shall sever you generously for this act of betrayal. Hear this, you miserable creature. You can run from me; hide in the most remote and furthest outreaches of the Galaxy, but I will find you." The Tyrant spat the words out. "Our paths will cross again, and when they do…"

The Tyrant flicked a button. The screen went blank. The Dread Lord gave a theatrical sigh. "Now where was I? Ah yes. The Server…" The Tyrant turned his attention back to the Bug still standing on the bridge.

"We can get The Server back," gabbled the Big Bug.

"Promises, promises." The Tyrant shook his head. "You are not going to have the opportunity. I will no longer tolerate your species' incompetence. I am suspending all Bug operations forthwith and sending all Bug agents into exile. All will return to the cloning moon of Nerdoofo, until further notice." The Tyrant's voice was as hard as boron. "I will not accept failure. Failure is not an option."

"Exile!" cried the Big Bug. "But that is not fair!"

"Fair is a word not in my dictionary – it is far too close to failure."

The Big Bug stood still, the gaping abyss yawning down either side of him. "What do I do now?" he demanded bitterly, gesturing at the bridge. "Do you expect me to walk?"

"No, Eric – I expect you to die."

The Tyrant hit a button on his console. The bridge tilted. For a second the Big Bug tried to balance on the thin metal, arms flailing like a scarecrow in a hurricane.

Then it dropped, screaming, into the abyss.

The scream lasted a very long time. It was followed by a faint splash and more – very faint, but enthusiastic – screaming.

There was silence.

The Tyrant turned back to his console and activated a hyper-link communication channel.

"Are the humans still on the planet Earth?"

"Yes." The slim figure answering the call had green skin and hair. "They're with the two chameleoids. I am monitoring their movements. Do you wish me to take The Server from them?"

"If you can." The Tyrant's voice was non-committal. "I have offered a reward for any being who brings me The Server. Even as we speak, several bounty hunters are heading for Earth by ship or teleportation, each hoping to claim the prize."

The caller gave an angry hiss. "But I am here already. I can get The Server. Don't you trust me?"

"I trust no one," The Tyrant said sharply. "I did not become the Dark Lord of the Galaxy by trusting anybody!"

The caller snorted. "Yet it seems you would entrust this mission to the most degenerate scum in the Galaxy."

"It takes one to know one," The Tyrant said mildly. "The more hunters there are, the more likely the success of the mission. If you wish to bring me The Server, then you may take your chance with everyone else."

The figure gave an angry nod. "What about the humans?"

The Evil Lord of the Galaxy didn't hesitate with his reply. "Eliminate them."

USAF Base, Little Slaughter, near Cambridge, England
"Kidnapped by aliens." The policeman stared at Jack. Then he flipped his notebook shut and folded his arms across it. "You'll have to do better than that, son."

"That's not what I said." Jack shook his head wearily. "You're not listening."

"Oh, Jack!" Jack's mother was perched on the very edge of the uncomfortable, government-issue chair she had been offered at the start of the interview. "Tell the truth, love. Please. Then we can go home." Jack's father sat next to her, looking at the floor in moody silence.

"Let's start again at the beginning." The policeman opened his notebook again and cast a sideways glance to check that the red light of the recording machine was still on. He was not a happy man. He wasn't happy to be on the United States Air Force base, in an unfamiliar interview room. He wasn't happy that his interview technique was being watched (and doubtless assessed) by Air Force security. He wasn't happy that Jack Armstrong had reappeared on the base instead of at his home, starting off all these procedural headaches. Above all, he wasn't happy that Jack, having disappeared ten days before with two Air force dependants – one of whom was the daughter of the base commander – wasn't telling a story that made any kind of sense.

Jack spread his hands on the bare tabletop. "I've already told you. We had to leave Earth to protect The Server…"

"This is the laptop computer which you say gets you on to the Galaxy-wide-web and sends you to lots of alien planets…" the policeman said woodenly.

"By teleportation, right!" Jack brightened. Maybe the policeman was starting to listen to him after all.

"Including one where you turned into a bear and your friend Merle Stone turned into a cat."

"No, you've got that wrong," said Jack helpfully. "Merle turned into a flying seal. Googie was a cat to start with, and she turned into a gazelle, but then she turned back into a cat again."

"Of course she did. I saw her myself an hour ago, she was definitely a cat then." The policeman gazed at Jack poker-faced. "And all this was to stop your computer falling into the hands of your enemies, the 'FOEs'. "

"Those that *have* hands, yes." Jack shuddered.

"And then you got sent back into the past, so you could tell some alien how to get this whole Galactic web thing started – even though it had to exist in order to send you back to start it."

"Er … yes." Jack was a bit unclear on that part himself.

"And now you've come back to Earth to wait for some alien to contact you with instructions on getting this computer – The 'Server' – to the leader of the 'Friends', called…" The policeman consulted his notes. "'The Weaver'?"

"You've got it." Jack nodded eagerly. His mother groaned softly.

The policeman rubbed one hand over his face. Either the kid was lying his socks off to cover up who-knew-what, or this was a job for the psychiatrists. He leaned forward. "Look, son, I hope you realize the seriousness of your situation."

As the policeman reeled off the probable consequences of continuing to give a false account of his absence, an air base security sergeant watched Jack with narrowed eyes. The kid's story had to be a pile of baloney. Except that there *had* been those reports of a two-headed alien life form on the base, and then Colonel Stone had started acting strangely, and then those two CIA men had shown up, except when they'd checked with the CIA they'd never heard of them. The sergeant wasn't an over-imaginative type, but there had been enough weird things going on at the base to make him wonder…

* * *

Some distance from the base police station, Merle was getting the third degree from her father.

She had expected Colonel Stone to put on his best parade-ground manner and give her the sort of dressing-down he reserved for airmen who'd turned up late for duty. But the reality was worse. Colonel Stone was being Reasonable, with a capital R. This was like being reasonable with a small r, except it clearly took a lot more effort. This made Merle very uncomfortable. She would have preferred it if her dad had started throwing furniture.

"I've tried to do the best I could for you," Colonel Stone was saying. Merle bit her lip. She hated it when her dad blamed himself for not bringing her up properly since her mother had died.

Colonel Stone stopped pacing the room and sat down on the edge of an armchair. This put him face to face with Merle, who was curled up on the sofa, running her dark fingers nervously through her braided hair and hugging a scatter-cushion. He looked directly into her eyes. Merle squirmed. Uh-oh. She was in for a man-to-man talk.

"I know exactly what's going on." Colonel Stone's voice was firm and measured. "You can't fool me." He began to tick points off on his fingers. "Strange computers that can send people to different planets. Two-headed aliens running around the base – creatures that can change their shape in the blink of an eye – time travel, parallel realities…" He paused, then said very quietly, "C'mon,

Merle, you can tell me the truth, and then we can start to work this thing out." He reached out and took her hand. "It's drugs, isn't it?'

"Dad!"

Merle's outraged protest sent Colonel Stone striding round the room. "Well, what then? Will you talk to me, for Pete's sake?"

Merle gazed at him, feeling amused, resentful and stricken with guilt at the same time. How could he think ... but then, the truth *was* kinda wild... Merle sighed inwardly. How could she square things with her dad when he'd never believe the true story of where she'd been? She wondered how the others were getting on – Jack, and Loaf, and Bitz.

The small brown and white mongrel with the lopsided ear stared at the mess of cereal and unidentifiable gristly tubes in his food bowl, and felt his stomach turn over. All round him, genuine dogs were wolfing down the disgusting offal that humans seemed to think dogs loved (And then they had the nerve to complain about how bad dogs' breath smelt. Sheesh!). Well, maybe real dogs *did* like this junk. The problem was, Bitz wasn't a real dog: he was a chameleoid – a shape-shifting alien life form. As Friends Agent Sirius, he'd had to get used to the feeding habits of the bodies that he'd assumed, and some of them had been pretty bizarre. For one assignment, he'd taken on the form of a Marman Megaphant Beetle, living on the dung of the Marman Megaphant (Bitz winced at the memory). But even then, the Megapahants hadn't manufactured the dung deliberately in the belief that the beetles *liked* it...

Bitz gave a low whine. Soon, dinner time would be over and then the other dogs in the pound would be back to growling, yapping, running round in circles for no particular reason. And play fighting – at least, he assumed that's what it was – though his left ear still ached from a scrap with an over-enthusiastic fox-terrier. Bitz actually enjoyed being a dog most of the time, but that was when he was around The Server whose translation programmes allowed him to communicate with humans. Humans were pretty dumb sometimes, but at least they could hold up their end of a conversation. The longest exchange of ideas Bitz had had since coming to the pound had been:

"Woof!"

"Woof?"

"Growl!"

"Whine?"

"Snarl!"

As Bitz sat lost in gloom, a nearby voice said, "Meow."

Meow? That wasn't something you heard a lot in the dog-pound.

Bitz casually looked round, then sidled nonchalantly over to the wire fence surrounding his prison. Googie sat primly on her haunches outside the wire. As Bitz edged closer, the cat-shaped chameleoid licked an elegant paw and smoothed down her ear. "Well, well," she said in the language of Kippo VI, her homeworld. "How are you? Having a nice time with all the other dumb mutts?"

Bitz was too depressed to give the cat an argument. "Humans!" he whined in Kippan accented with the nasal twang of Usnan, the language of his own planet in the Epsilon sector. "We save the Galaxy, and what do they do? Lock me up in this place! I could tell you stories ... there's this Dobermann." Bitz shivered, then glared at Googie. "Hey! How come you get to roam around like you own the place while I'm cooped up in the slammer?"

"It's perfectly simple," drawled Googie. "I am an independent, self-willed, free-spirited cat: while you are an untrustworthy, car-chasing, pavement-fouling, pants-sniffing, ankle-biting, gatepost-peeing brute of a dog – that's why!"

Bitz bared his teeth. "Is zat so?" He turned his head and gave a yap. Heads emerged from dinner bowls. Tails went up. A cat!

Half a second later, the wire fence was thrumming from an assault of scrabbling claws. Snarling muzzles were drawn back over snapping teeth as dogs of all shapes and sizes tore at the wire to get at Googie. The cat sat washing herself, secure in the knowledge that the worst they could do was make her eardrums ache.

She rose to her feet. "See you around," she told Bitz, "when you come up for parole, maybe. I'm glad to see you among companions of your own intellectual level." With that, she paced off, deliberately staying close to the wire but just out of reach. The dogs in the pound kept pace with her, still throwing themselves at the wire in a useless snarling frenzy.

Bitz sighed. Maybe he should have been a bit more diplomatic. He hadn't asked Googie how the humans were getting on, or what had happened to The Server...

"Groof!"

Bitz felt several drops of slobber land on his shoulder. He looked up, into the grinning muzzle of a large Dobermann.

Bitz's ears drooped. "Oh, brother!" he muttered to himself.

Space Trading Post 478, Trojan Sector

Halfway across the Galaxy, a droop-shouldered figure sat on a cracked plastic stool in a seedy spacer bar, wondering how long he could spin out drinking an already-cold cup of Cassiopeian cappuccino before the hard-eyed proprietor threw him out. Zodiac Hobo was down on his luck, and a long way from home.

The bottom had fallen out of the space-desperado business. Nobody seemed to want any illegal cargoes running these days, and there wasn't a merchant in the

Galaxy dumb enough to trust Zodiac with the legal sort. Seeing the barkeep swivel a suspicious antenna-top eyeball in his direction, Zodiac hurriedly took a sip of mud-flavoured froth and wiped his green beard with a six-fingered hand that was even grubbier than usual. His beloved solar flares were covered with food stains, his space-boots were down at heel, and a colony of Muscan Munching Moths had reduced the frills on his shirt to ribbons.

The bar where Zodiac sat feeling sorry for himself was on the worst habitat-level of Space Trading Post 478 in the Trojan Sector. He was sitting there drinking endless cups of terrible coffee, because he had nowhere else to go. He had been forced to put into the station when the engines of his ship, *Trigger*, had started producing dense clouds of blue smoke. When he'd asked his ship's brain what the problem was, he'd immediately wished he hadn't.

"What's the problem? What's the problem?" Trigger had immediately flown into a string of tearful reproaches. *"What do you expect? You buy cheap fuel, you never do any maintenance checks, you just take me for granted..."*

With Trigger's complaints ringing in his ears, Zodiac had brought his ship limping into the station at Whoosh Factor One, only to have his vessel impounded for previous non-payment of docking fees.

The barkeep writhed over to Zodiac's table on its numerous flagella, which undulated beneath it like the bristles of an animate rotary floor-polisher. The green-skinned being wiped Zodiac's table with a filthy cloth, arranging the dirt into streaks. Zodiac looked up with a guilty start. "Yeah – hey, dude, this is great coffee, y'know? Like, you gotta drink it slow to get the full flavour."

"Can it, creep." As far as the barkeep was concerned, customer care was something that happened to other life-forms. "There's somebody wants to see ya."

Elephant ears unfolded either side of the barkeep's back. Their owner emerged, and after a moment's sight-less fumbling put a hand on Zodiac's shoulder. Then another hand. And then another four.

"Zodiac Hobo," hissed Tracer.

Zodiac's orange skin turned an unhealthy shade of yellow. "Oh, man!" he groaned. "I told you on Helios, I don't want to get involved in any heavy scene. Like, why d'you want to come here buggin' me?"

"Shut up!" Two of Tracer's claws produced a small wad of notes and he tipped the barkeep, who moved away after a final unpleasant leer at Zodiac. Tracer transferred another two hands to Zodiac's collar. He twisted it in a grip of surprising strength as he slid into the seat next to Zodiac.

Tracer's skin was still blistered from the burst of plasma energy he had suffered on the planet Helios in his attempt to break the connection between The Server and the great semi-organic computer, Tiresias. Zodiac stared at the burnt-out visor he had last seen pulsing with light as it fed information to The Tyrant's all seeing Chief of Surveillance, and waved a hand in front of it. "Hooo, dude, what happened to the old peek-a-roonie? Looks like you couldn't even get cable on that thing."

Tracer's grip tightened. Zodiac sputtered into silence. "Spare me your imbecilities," rasped the elephant-eared being. As Zodiac gasped for breath, Tracer relaxed and his rat-trap mouth curled into a sneer. "From what I hear, you're not doing so well yourself."

Zodiac massaged his throat. "Hey, man, you know how it goes," he squeaked with ill-feigned nonchalance. "You win some, you lose some."

"It sounds to me as if you've been losing most of them lately." Tracer gave Zodiac his shoulder back. "Do you want a job?"

Zodiac groaned. "No way, dude. Like, I don't do government contracts, you know that…"

"For reasons that do not concern you," Tracer interrupted him, "at the moment I am on what you might call detached duty…"

Zodiac's multicoloured eyes narrowed shrewdly. "Had a bust-up with the Big Guy, eh?"

Tracer ignored the interruption. "I have your ship," he said casually. "I bought it this morning. I could find another pilot, and put into effect the one hundred and forty-six arrest warrants that remain outstanding against your name."

Zodiac closed his eyes. "Or?" he said tonelessly.

"Or I could have your ship repaired, and you can have it back and be free to go anywhere in the Galaxy you want." Tracer's voice became a harsh growl. "Provided it's Earth."

"You want me to go to Earth?" Zodiac stirred unhappily on his stool. "Oh, man, I'm getting bad vibes about this…"

USAF Base, Little Slaughter, near Cambridge, England

In the living room of a house on the US Air Force base, Loaf was facing a slavering, red-faced creature whose throbbing purple veins stood out above bloodshot eyes that bulged almost out of its head. It wasn't much of a comfort to Loaf that the creature in question was his father.

"I had my credit card statement yesterday." Master Sergeant Gelt's voice had the rasping quality of a badly-oiled chainsaw. "It seems I owe fifty billion US dollars to some loan-shark company I've never heard of. I don't suppose you'd happen to know anything about that?"

Fortunately for Loaf, at that moment all the windows blew in.

2

Sirens wailed. Every street on the air base was filled with running figures – officers and airmen heading for their duty stations, their families rushing for cover. Frank Stone, struggling into a flak jacket, wrenched open the front door of his house and hit the lawn running just as a jeep skidded to a halt outside. The colonel vaulted into the passenger seat and turned to glare at Merle as she hopped in the back. "Where d'you think you're going?"

Merle gave him back look for look. "I'm coming to Operations with you."

"You're going to the shelter!"

Merle shook her head. "You need me. The Book doesn't cover what's happening here." She pointed into the sky. "Have you seen what's bombing us?"

Frank Stone followed his daughter's pointing finger and gaped.

Overhead, a craft that looked like a silver running shoe tore across the sky. It was followed by something that looked like a flying steam iron with torpedo-shaped outriggers. Both vessels fired energy weapons at something out of sight behind the base houses. Whatever they hit went "Crump!" There was a lot of smoke.

"What on Earth..." Her father turned an incredulous face to Merle. "No. Cancel that. Nothing *on Earth.* Friends of yours?"

Merle shook her head. "Far from it. This is a close encounter of the fourth kind."

Her father stared. "The fourth kind?"

Merle ducked as a horseshoe-shaped craft powered overhead. "Yeah – that's where the aliens shoot at you."

Colonel Stone hitched up his jaw. "OK. You're with me. There's a steel helmet under your seat. Put it on."

The jeep set off with a squeal of rubber. Merle found the helmet and made a face. It weighed a tonne. It would play *havoc* with her hair.

Something like a flying motorcycle shot overhead. The road in front of them exploded. The jeep swerved violently. Merle put the helmet on.

Across the base, Loaf – his face bleeding where he had been cut by flying glass – scrabbled desperately at the door handle of his dad's motor home.

"Siddown," snarled Master Sergeant Gelt, hauling at the wheel of the cumbersome vehicle to send it yawing violently around a crater.

"Dad!" Loaf's face was white with fear. "Shouldn't we

be heading for the shelter? I mean, it's *dangerous* out there. What are you doing?"

"Protecting my investment!"

"What investment? Dad, you can't be serious! I know you're into wheeling and dealing in a big way, but it's Air Force property the aliens are destroying. All these airplanes and trucks and stuff belong to the US government – they don't belong to you!"

The Master Sergeant glared at his son. "Wanna bet?"

Before Loaf could reply, a movement in the rear-view mirror caught his eye. He screamed like a cat with its tail caught in a slamming door.

Something that looked like a flying gyroscope zeroed in on the outsized camper. There was a flash of light, and the body of the monstrous vehicle exploded into shards of composition board, aluminium sheeting and tasteless upholstery.

Now driving little more than a flatbed truck with no back to its cab, Master Sergeant Gelt cast a livid look at his gibbering son. "That's coming out of *your* allowance!"

Bitz made for the gap in the wire where a speeding car had powered straight through; its driver had been distracted by a horseshoe-shaped alien spacecraft crossing the road in front of it. Behind him, a whimpering Dobermann was trying to hide underneath an upturned kennel. Bitz reached the gap. He paused, went back into

the pound, and bit the Dobermann savagely on the leg.
Then he headed for the centre of the excitement as fast
as his short legs could carry him.

"Look, Sergeant! I have to get to Colonel Stone."

Jack was finding it difficult to stay calm. Apart from the
bombardment, his mother and father were trying to drag
him under the interview room table to shelter.

The sergeant, holding his sidearm as if not quite sure
what to do with it, turned from the window. "This is a
combat situation, mister! There's nothing in the rule book
that says suspects in detention get to see the
Commanding Officer."

"What does the rule book say about what to do if the
base is attacked by alien spacecraft?"

The sergeant grimaced. The kid had a point. On the
other hand, if he let a suspect out of custody without
authorization, he'd probably be busted to Airman Third
Class In Charge Of Latrines.

A movement outside the window caught his eye. A
three-metre reptilian alien wearing bronze armour was
striding towards the detention block. It was carrying what
was almost certainly an energy weapon the size of a
steam locomotive. The sergeant swung round. "On the
floor," he snapped. "Cover your heads."

The policeman, who had been trying without success
to contact his inspector by mobile phone in search of

further instructions, glared at the security man. "Don't give me orders," he said tightly. "I am a member of the British police…"

"Good for you." The sergeant jerked his head towards the window. "Why don't you arrest *him?*"

The policeman said nothing. He reached inside his jacket and pulled out a small leather wallet. Then, before the sergeant's incredulous gaze, he squared his shoulders and marched out of the door.

Standing on the steps of the detention block, the policeman held out his warrant-card like a very inadequate shield, and said in a ringing voice, "I'm arresting you on charges of affray, causing a public nuisance and wilful damage to property. You're not obliged to say anything, but…"

Recovering from his astonishment, the sergeant shoulder-charged the policeman to the ground and dropped into a firing stance. He emptied a full clip of ammunition at the alien.

Some invisible force around the alien sparkled. Spent slugs dropped harmlessly to the road. The sergeant gulped. The alien gave him a wicked grin, and raised its weapon.

The sergeant dived to one side just in time.

When he had recovered sufficiently from the near miss, the sergeant staggered to his feet, turned – and let out a hollow groan.

His prisoner, and his prisoner's parents had disappeared. So had the detention block.

"What's the story, Hal?"

Colonel Stone strode into the operations room with Merle at his heels. Major Hal Jackson, the colonel's aide, wasted no time questioning her arrival.

"There are at least a dozen vessels attacking us," he said crisply. "Maybe more. They're moving so fast it's hard to keep count. There seem to be other attackers using some kind of jet-packs or anti-gravity devices, fly-cycles…" Jackson's voice rose as he shrugged helplessly. "We don't even have *words* for the hardware these guys are using…"

Colonel Stone was staring at the status board. "Defences?"

The major regained his composure. "We had time to scramble a couple of F15s, but they were downed after reporting complete systems failure. Pilots ejected. The other birds' engines won't even fire up. We managed to get off some surface-to-air missiles, but they exploded well before reaching their targets. Apart from that, we're down to semi-automatic weapons and throwing rocks."

"Have we informed U.S.A.F. H.Q? The Pentagon?"

Jackson shook his head. "We have a compete communications blackout. Radio, all frequencies; landlines, computers, cell and satellite phones; everything's down."

"Dad." Merle's voice was calm but insistent. "You know who they're after – and what."

Colonel Stone said nothing. Locked in the most secure safe the base could provide – along with some very important keys and envelopes containing instructions and codes that Colonel Stone didn't even want to think about – was an ordinary-looking (more or less) laptop computer. The colonel hadn't believed Merle's story that this device was in truth a staggeringly sophisticated alien communications device called The Server, but he hadn't reached command rank in the world's largest air force by taking unnecessary risks.

"Merle!" A wild-eyed boy of Merle's age had ducked past the MPs guarding the door and now had her by the arms, shaking her. "These aliens are after The Server. If they don't get it, they'll wreck the base. We could get seriously killed!"

The MPs caught up with Loaf and dragged him away from Merle just as Master Sergeant Carl Gelt appeared, gasping for breath and smouldering slightly. He gave a sketchy salute. "Reporting for duty, sir!"

"At ease, Sergeant." Colonel Stone gave Loaf an unfriendly glance. "Restrain your son. Sit on him if necessary."

"I'm afraid Loaf's right, sir."

Colonel Stone's face grew livid as he glared at the shock-headed, untidily dressed kid and his nervous-looking parents, who must have come in while the MPs' attention was on Loaf. As a British citizen, a civilian – and a minor – Jack Armstrong had absolutely no business at all in Ops, but he carried himself with an air of quiet authority that suggested he had. "Colonel," Jack went on, "the aliens are here for the Server – and probably for me, Merle and Loaf as well." His mother put a protective hand on Jack's shoulder, which he gently removed. "We've been telling you the truth, Colonel. I don't blame you for not believing us, but right now the truth really *is* out there, and the FOEs will go on tearing your base apart just as long as they know we're here."

The colonel bit back the stinging response his training and everything he believed were prompting him to make. Instead, he proved that he was worth his exalted rank by saying, "What do you suggest?"

Space Trading Post 478, Trojan Sector

The Cyclopian Customs and Immigration Officer looked up from the desk, which was covered with forms it was filling out with infuriating slowness. He gave Zodiac Hobo an unfriendly look. Zodiac wasn't fazed by this. Cyclopians gave *everyone* unfriendly looks.

The Cyclopian transferred the intimidating gaze of its single unblinking eye on to Zodiac's suitcase. It was a large, cheap pressed-fibre model, and from the way Zodiac was struggling with it, obviously very heavy.

Zodiac put the case down (the Cyclopian wondered for a moment whether he could possibly have heard a muffled "Ooof!" from inside) and slapped a semi-transparent plastic flimsy down on the desk in front of the intimidating official. "Release form," he said cheerfully. "Filled in and signed in octuplicate. This certifies that I've paid off all outstanding fees and am free to leave this facility." He grinned at the charmless official. "Like, parting is such sweet sorrow, dude."

The Cyclopian gave a disappointed grunt, on general principles, and checked the form with maddening slowness. Eventually, it reluctantly conceded that everything seemed to be in order and Zodiac was free to go.

Zodiac produced another form. "Clearance application for passage to Earth, dude."

"Earth?" The Cyclopian narrowed its eye suspiciously. "Why Earth?"

Zodiac gave a careless shrug. "I hear The Tyrant is looking for bounty hunters for a short but well-paid assignment. Like, I've decided to try my luck."

The Cyclopian gave Zodiac a contemptuous look. "You don't look like a bounty hunter to me."

"Better believe it, dude." Zodiac gave the Cyclopian an outrageous wink. "I specialize in secret missions."

The Cyclopian sniffed contemptuously. "I've never heard of you."

Zodiac gave him a big friendly grin. "See? That's how

good I am. Licensed to kill, thrill and chill."

"I'll have to get authorization for this." The Cyclopian picked up the form and lumbered off, through a door marked "Private".

"Don't overdo it!" said Zodiac's suitcase in complaining tones. "I thought you were going to blow the whole deal."

Zodiac shook the case with unnecessary force. "You OK in there, man?"

"Ow! No thanks to you. And don't call me 'man'!"

"Don't sweat it."

"I am not, as you so charmingly put it, 'sweating it'." Tracer's voice was muffled. "Which is more than I can say for your socks."

Zodiac kicked the case in warning as the Cyclopian returned. "Passage approved," it grunted with reluctance. Then its eye took on an unpleasant glint. "What's in the case?"

Zodiac replied, cheerfully, "My underwear." He paused slightly. "Used."

The Cyclopian looked hard at Zodiac. It took in the soiled flares, the moth-eaten shirt, the tangled beard and the straggly hair…

…And hurriedly stamped "CHECKED" on the suitcase. Zodiac made his way to the embarkation lock, whistling all the way.

USAF Base, Little Slaughter, near Cambridge, England

The Server sat on a side table of the Ops room with all the baleful innocence of an unexploded grenade.

Colonel Stone stared at it. "That's what this is all about?"

Jack nodded. "Help."

Colonel Stone drew back with a sharp intake of breath as the hologram of The Server's unreliable Help application appeared floating in its customary place above the device's keyboard. *"Now you want Help! You let me be snatched by a bunch of know-nothing primates, and locked in some miserable vault, do you know how bad that is for my claustrophobia?"*

"Complain later," Jack told it. "You're on the Air Force base. Who's attacking us?"

"Always the questions!" Help complained. *"Lemme monitor recent o-mail announcements."* After a slight pause it continued, *"The Tyrant has retired the Bugs."*

Loaf gave a relieved whistle. "Good."

"Not good," snapped Help. *"He's sicked bounty hunters on you instead. They're not as strong as Bugs, but they're twice as sneaky. And they're motivated by the most powerful force in the Galaxy…"*

"Money," said Merle bitterly.

"You got it."

At that moment, a scruffy mongrel dog and an aristocratic-looking cat, whose fur had a distinctive blue tinge, slid into the room.

"Hi, Jack," growled Bitz. "What's the plan?"

Googie leaped on to the table beside The Server. "Why are you all sitting around? Don't you feel we should be getting out of here?"

Major Jackson gave a hollow groan. "Talking dogs and cats. Now I've seen everything!" Colonel Stone shook his head in disbelief.

The building shook as a blast from an alien weapon detonated nearby.

"Googie's right," said Merle. "The bounty hunters are after *us* and The Server, not the base. Get ready to teleport."

"But teleporting will give our position away," protested Loaf.

Merle gave him a scornful look. "I think they already *know* our position!" She bent over The Server and began to punch at the keys. "I'll try and input some coordinates."

"Where to?" said Jack.

"Anywhere other than here…"

"Just a minute, young lady!" roared Colonel Stone. "You aren't going anywhere."

"Don't worry, Dad," Merle gave her father a big, winning smile. "I have my phone, so you can keep in touch and…."

She was interrupted by a commotion in the corridor outside. Two MPs darted into the Operations room, slamming the heavy steel door behind them. A rhythmic electronic throbbing noise sounded from the other side of the door, which was glowing bright yellow. Sparkling motes of light appeared in the middle of the door, forming a whirlpool pattern – like water draining down a bath plug – with a void at its centre. The vortex spread. Within seconds the door had disappeared.

As the startled security men stepped back, a nightmarish alien creature slithered through the empty doorframe, twitching violently and waving horrendous-looking weapons in all directions.

"Uh-oh." Help immediately disappeared into the relative safety of The Server. A sign appeared on its screen.

closeD dVe to CowaRdiCe.

"Make any sudden moves you want," screeched the intruder. It gave an insane cackle. Its four bloodshot eyes rotated crazily in different directions. "Do something stupid, and everybody'll get hurt. I'm gonna kill ya! I'm gonna kill ya!"

3

Deep Space

Zodiac jabbed at a tiny wire. "How about this?"

"Zeeuuuaaaarrghhh!!!" Tracer's eight limbs shot out into a "dead starfish" position and his ears went rigid.

Zodiac gave a sheepish grin. "So ... not that one then?"

"Mr Hobo," said Tracer through clenched teeth. "Do not do that again ... or I will hurt you very badly."

Zodiac nodded. "I dig your lick, dude."

As *Trigger* sped through the blackness of deep space en route to Earth, Tracer had insisted that Zodiac make an attempt to fix his burnt-out VR visor. This was turning out not to be one of his better decisions. Zodiac was to DIY what The Tyrant was to Galactic peace and harmony.

"Very well, let us continue." Tracer wiped sweat from his brow and shook his ears. "Now ... *making sure you don't touch what you touched last time* ... attach the pink plasma diode to the purple wire."

Zodiac gave a low groan. "Ohhh, man. Ain't no point in talking about colours to a Jivan – we see everything in all the colours of the rainbow, all the time."

Tracer gave a deep sigh. "Having seen your dress sense, I might have guessed."

Zodiac completed the connection. Tracer's visor fizzed, and burst into fitful life. Light pulsed intermittently across the black plastic.

"Yoh! Sparkly," whooped Zodiac, punching the air. "Am I the daddy or what!"

Tracer frowned. "Mr Hobo, are you by any chance standing on your head?"

Zodiac looked puzzled. "No, dude."

"Then you've wired my visor incorrectly, you fool!" screamed Tracer. "Everything is upside down!"

A few more minutes of ham-fisted fiddling with the visor's circuitry, and Tracer finally gave a satisfied, "Enough, it's working." He looked about, taking in the less-than-luxurious surroundings. "This ship can actually fly? Incredible."

Trigger sniffed. *"Charming."*

Tracer checked the navigation display. "But we are still several hundred light years from Earth."

Zodiac slapped his thigh. "Bummer! Then we aren't gonna get to this party on time. All the cake will have been eaten."

"I think we will."

Zodiac shook his head. "No way, daddio. Even if we travel at Whoosh Factor Fifty, which Trigger ain't close to being able to do, we'll still take years. So how you planning to get there – t-mail?"

Tracer shook his head decisively. "The Tyrant will be closely monitoring all Earth-bound t-mails. The minute we tried to teleport to Earth, we would be diverted to Kazamblam or even worse, to the Dark Pyramid. We're going to take a short cut."

"A short cut?" Zodiac thought for a second. Then he grinned and winked broadly at Tracer. "Like, are you thinking of taking Trigger through a worm hole? Haaaaaa, haaaa, haaa, ha, h…" Zodiac's laugh died on his lips as he caught sight of Tracer's unsmiling face. "Oh man, you are kidding me."

Trigger gave a high pitched wail. *"Worm holes!"*

"You have rocks in your head," moaned Zodiac. "Using worm holes as a form of interstellar travel is crazy dangerous."

"No, it's simple." Tracer's voice was matter-of-fact. "We steer into the mouth of a worm hole, travel through it and emerge at the other end of the hole. Thus we cut through time and space and end up in the Sol System very near to Earth."

"What if this mouth eats us? Come on dude," pleaded Zodiac. "This trip sounds like one big downer. I reckon we should vote on this crazy idea."

"I'm against it!" said Trigger immediately. *"Anyway, I don't want to help you chase the humans – especially*

the one called Merle. She was nice to me. She gave me my name. She didn't make me go through nasty worm holes..."

"Operationally challenged ships' brains don't have a vote!" interrupted Tracer.

"Fascist!" sniffed Trigger.

Tracer ignored the comment. "Organic life forms against using a worm hole?"

Both Zodiac's hands shot up.

"Those for." One by one, Tracer slowly raised all six of his arms. He smiled. "You're outvoted by six to two."

"Hey, no way, José. Man, that is so not fair," protested Zodiac. "Limbs are not democratic, otherwise Munervian Millipedes would always get elected. Come on, Tracer, dude, there's one of me and one of you."

Tracer gave a considered nod. "You're right of course. We need a casting vote." He reached into the depths of his jacket, pulled out a lethal-looking energy weapon and pointed it at the space hippy's head.

Zodiac shifted uncomfortably in his seat. "Oh man. Motion passed."

USAF Base, Little Slaughter, near Cambridge, England
The alien bounty hunter stood framed in the hole formerly known as a door, twitching uncontrollably. Its bright yellow skin glowed in the harsh neon light of the Ops room. Glistening fangs protruded from both its slavering

mouths. It was covered in leather from head to lower tentacle, with leather cross-belts and matching leather accessories.

Jack's mother gave a little scream. "It's horrible!"

"Yeah." Merle shuddered. "Leather is *soooo* passé."

"Take it out." Colonel Stone's harsh command rang out through the horrified silence. But before the guards could raise their rifles, the creature fired. A blue bolt of plasma energy lit up the room, momentarily blinding everyone. The guards blinked in astonishment as their guns melted in their hands.

The being's eyes spun with evil delight. "Next time, I set it to disintegrate *you*. I'll melt ya all!"

The colonel gestured to his men. "Take it easy and back off."

The bounty hunter pointed several of his weapons at the companions. "Where izzz it? Where izzz it?" it hissed from one of its mouths.

Bitz padded forward. He stood between the hunter and Jack. "Where's what, ugly?"

The creature turned its maniacal eyes on the chameleoid. "Don't make me mad, don't make me mad! They don't call me Mad Moxie for nothing! If I get mad, you'll regret it."

Merle cast a furtive glance at The Server. "Can't he see it?" she hissed to Jack.

"He doesn't know what it looks like," Jack whispered

back. "The Server can look like anything it wants, remember?"

"I programmed the teleport," breathed Merle. "All I have to do is press 'Send', but if I touch The Server he'll spot it..."

Mad Moxie gave a squeal of rage. "Enough talking! I want The Server! Gimme, gimme, gimme!"

Bitz bared his teeth. "You don't scare us," he growled.

"Yes it does," whimpered Loaf. "A lot."

Steam poured from Mad Moxie's three nostrils. "You're making me mad. You won't like me when I'm mad."

Bitz snarled. "I'm not crazy about you *now*."

Jack's father stepped forward, his eyes glinting with anger. "See here, Mister. I don't like your manners and I don't like the way you come barging in here threatening my family."

Jack gulped. His father was talking to this psychopathic alien, just as if he were castigating Jack for not doing the washing up.

Mad Moxie twitched even more. "Ohhhh! You just made me mad. You shouldn't have done that!" He turned several of his weapons on Jack's father. Steam shot from his nostrils, his eyes spun uncontrollably. "I'm gonna kill ya, I'm gonna kill ya!"

BLAM!

Mad Moxie's four eyes stopped spinning. The creature looked down at the hole in his chest. "Hey, somebody's gone and killed me." It toppled over and lay still.

"Howdee."

A tall, thin humanoid with bright blue eyes blazing out of an almost translucent face stood at the doorway. It wore a simple cloth poncho draped over its shoulders. It blew at the muzzle of a smoking energy pistol and drawled, "They call me The Thing with No Name."

Jack sighed with relief. "You got here just in time, Mister ... um ... Thing. Thank you."

"That 'thank you' might be a little premature," rasped the creature. "I've come for The Server."

"What Server?" asked Jack, innocently.

The Thing's eyes narrowed to mere slits. "The Server that's translating every word you and I say... The black box that the lady is trying to hide behind her back."

Merle looked desperately towards Jack. He shrugged helplessly.

"Merle," ordered Colonel Stone, "give him The Server."

"But Dad!" protested Merle. "The future of the Galaxy..."

"Do it!" her father snapped.

"Glad to see someone has some sense around these parts." The Thing with No Name held out a seven-fingered hand.

"Hold it right there!" A commanding voice rang out across the Ops room.

"Not more aliens," moaned Loaf. "I'm dosed up on alien life forms."

The new arrival was a female humanoid, over two metres tall, with green skin and spiky hair the colour and texture of grass. She wore a skin-tight one-piece black outfit in some shiny material. She was only carrying a single energy weapon, but she looked as if she knew how to use it.

"Tingkat Bumbag!" The Thing with No Name swung his energy pistol round to cover the new arrival.

Loaf snickered. "Tingkat Bumbag?"

The green-skinned woman gave Loaf a look that made the laughter die in his throat. "That's my name. Do you find it amusing?" Frantically, Loaf shook his head.

The Thing with No Name faced Tingkat squarely. "Sorry, Tingkat. You may be top gun hunter in the Galaxy, but according to the Rules of Bounty Hunting – paragraph seventeen, section three-zero-eight, clause six: *first come, first served.*"

Tingkat held up a long green finger. "But you're forgetting the Number One rule."

The Thing's brow creased in puzzlement. "What's that?"

BLAM!

The Thing slumped to the floor. Tingkat lowered her gun. "Paragraph one, section one, clause one: *The being who shoots first, wins.*" She turned to the humans. "And now, I'll have The Server if you please."

"If we hand it over to you, what happens to us?" asked

Jack, trying to stall for time.

"The Tyrant wants you," replied Tingkat, "dead or not alive."

Loaf looked puzzled. "Don't you mean dead or alive?"

Tingkat shook her head. "No, he was quite specific about that point. He's a very vindictive being. Give me The Server."

Merle and Jack exchanged glances. Merle held out The Server. As Tingkat lowered her weapon to take her prize, Merle's hand darted across The Server's keyboard and hit the "Send" key. The room was filled with an explosion of blue and white light and noise. Then there was silence.

Every human in the Ops room stared at the empty space which, a moment before, had held three teenagers, a cat and a dog. With a cry of rage, Tingkat raised her weapon, aimed it at the remaining humans – and lowered it again. "I should kill you for this insult!" she hissed. "But perhaps you will be of use later."

With that, she stepped over the bodies of the two ex-bounty-hunters and stalked out, leaving Colonel Stone and his men wide-eyed and shaking and Jack's mother and father hugging each other in relief.

Deep Space

"Is that it?" asked Zodiac, staring out of Trigger's view port at the swirling mass of energy. "That's the entrance to the worm hole?"

"Yes," replied Tracer. "And the opposite end of the hole brings us out near to Earth and The Server – which will soon be mine."

Zodiac stared at the writhing hole. It seemed almost alive. "I heard, at the end of every worm hole, there's a pot of enriched plutonium," he said dreamily. "Is that true?"

"No."

Zodiac gave a disappointed sigh. "Why is it called a worm hole anyway?" he asked.

"You'll find out," replied Tracer.

Flopping back into his seat, Zodiac gulped. "Am I going to like finding out?"

"Probably not."

Zodiac gave a moan and shut his eyes tightly.

"Set coordinates," Tracer commanded.

"*C-c-co-ord-d-d-inates set-t-t,*" stammered Trigger.

"Whoosh Factor Ten."

With a scream, Trigger roared into the gaping mouth of the worm hole. Zodiac's body was thrust into his seat. "Whhaaahhhh! Is this going to work?" he squealed.

Tracer's visor pulsed red. "Of course it is. Trust me."

N-Space

"I'm back home!" Bitz wagged his tail in glee. "Usnan III – my home planet!"

The companions had rematerialized in a huge plastic

dome, with antiseptic white floors. Clear pipes, filled with multi-coloured liquids, lined the walls. They looked like giant lava lamps – bubbles formed and glooped inside the ducts. Small clouds of steam hung in the air.

Bitz breathed in deeply. "It's good to be back."

Jack shook his head. "I don't think you *are* back. Look outside."

The dome seemed to be floating in a stream of rain-bow particles that flowed up, down and round in ever changing patterns.

"We're in N-Space again," said Jack as a familiar bald-headed figure materialized before the Friends. "Hello, Janus!"

The former Friends agent regarded them solemnly with his yellow eyes. "Greetings to you all."

Bitz gave a joyful yap. "You created this setting from my mind. Thanks, Janus."

"I'm surprised he found anything at all in *your* mind," muttered Googie.

Bitz gave her a hard stare.

"So this is what your planet looks like?" Jack gave Bitz a surprised look. "It's so clean! I'd never have believed you were from such a world." Jack caught Bitz's offended look. "I mean, you're … sort of scruffy…"

"Why do you think I'm not too keen on this body I'm stuck in?" growled Bitz. "Oh, for a germ-free environment!"

Merle turned on Janus. "I didn't program The Server to bring us here! You keep doing this to us! Ever since you wound up here in N-Space, you drag us in here whenever you want, like we were your puppets or something."

Janus shook his head resignedly. "Merle, will you never forgive me for making you abandon Lothar?"

Merle said nothing. Their last meeting with Janus had been an unhappy one, involving time travel, parallel realities and meeting Loaf's alternative self, a brave heroic, Lothar Gelt. Travelling back in time in order to help create The Outernet, they had taken Lothar from his reality on an alternate Earth and left him behind, a hundred years in the past, on the forest planet Vered II.

"Considering your predicament," continued Janus, "this seemed to me to be an opportune moment for us to meet."

"Last time we met you," Loaf complained, "you sent us back to Earth and told us to wait until we were contacted."

"You were," Janus pointed out.

"By a bunch of alien weapon-toting psychos!" exclaimed Loaf in exasperation.

"I did not say *who* would contact you…"

Loaf shook his head. "Whooo! You are more slippery than my old man!"

Jack took The Server from Merle and held it to his chest. "Why have you brought us here again, Janus?"

"I had to," explained Janus. "The FOEs have placed a divert to send any t-mail originating on Earth straight to the deepest dungeon in The Tyrant's Dark Pyramid. Had I not intercepted your teleport, The Tyrant would already have you and The Server at his mercy."

"Which in his case," muttered Bitz, "he has not got."

"But the bounty hunters are after us!" snapped Loaf. "How are we supposed to stay ahead of them? They've got space ships and big zappy weapon things that are going to be very bad for our health. The net is closing in on us."

Janus shook his head. "A net is just a series of holes. You can get through them. You will use teleportation to escape and keep ahead of these hunters."

Merle clenched her fists. "But you just said…"

Janus held up a hand. "Let me explain. There is a tele-portation system on Earth that predates Outernet tech-nology, but you have to be in the right place to use it. There are five such sites, one on each continent."

"Ancient Sites!" Bitz tried to slap his forehead with his paw, and missed. "Why didn't I think of that?"

"There are six continents," Merle pointed out. She counted them off on her fingers. "Americas, Europe, Africa, Asia, Oceania and Antarctica. Six."

"You are right, but the one on Antarctica has long van-ished. Even without it, the remaining sites are still able to maintain the Link. It was called Atlantis."

Bitz nodded. "Pity about the accident."

Merle curled her lip. "Atlantis? An accident? You're kidding me."

"Humans!" said Googie. "They never could resist meddling with elemental forces."

"Nobody knows," Janus said, "whether such sites were left by technologically advanced natives of the planets on which they are found, who have since disappeared, or whether they were built by alien visitors in older times. Each site retains many hidden powers. One of these is the power to teleport between the sites."

"So it's just like t-mail?" asked Loaf.

Janus shook his head. "Only in the sense that riding a broomstick is like flying in an airliner."

"Draughtier," added Bitz, "a lot more risky, plus you don't get an in-flight movie."

Janus continued his explanation. "In each location, you must initiate the site's defences by identifying and pressing a symbol before moving on to the next. The combined power of all the surviving sites will create an ancient defence against invasion." Janus paused for a second. "They will form a kind of primitive but powerful Chain around the planet. This will evict the bounty hunters from Earth and prevent any more invaders from arriving."

"So what you're saying," said Loaf sarcastically. "Is that it's up to us to save the Galaxy." He rolled his eyes theatrically. "Again."

4

Near Saturn, Sol System

Zodiac's ship shot through a hole in the black fabric of the sky. Trigger was looking very much the worse for wear.

Inside, Zodiac sat wide-eyed, his mouth opening and shutting like that of a large koi carp. He gave a cry that was no more than a breath. "The horror! The horror!"

Tracer rubbed his claws together. "There now, that wasn't so bad was it? Admittedly, some of those worms were a trifle playful and their seventeen sets of teeth can be a little disconcerting, but all in all, I'd say it was a good trip."

"*I want my motherboard!*" cried Trigger, bursting into tears.

Ignoring the blubbering spaceship, Tracer plotted their position. Several hundred thousand kilometres away on Trigger's starboard side was a huge planet, surrounded by three rings of icy particles, dust and other space debris. Tracer checked its coordinates. A planet called Saturn. Good. Tracer gave a smile. He wandered over to the view panel and looked out, searching for a distant speck in the blackness. He found it. "Earth…" he muttered to himself. And what was the name of the country on a small island? The answer came to him. Ah yes … England…

USAF Base, Little Slaughter, near Cambridge, England
Tingkat strode across the deserted airfield towards her space ship. What little resistance there had been to the hunters had been broken. Most of the air base personnel were lying low and taking shelter from the alien invaders. Since the first wave of attacks, dozens of hunters had appeared. The Tyrant's message had been well and truly received, Tingkat reflected sourly. All the scum and dregs of the Galaxy had made their way to this small planet, hoping for the big payday. She had beaten them all to the prize, but The Server had slipped from her fingers. What to do next, she wondered.

Her wrist communicator buzzed. She flicked it open and poked at it with a long green finger.

"You do not appear to be doing very well in your mission."

Tingkat recognized the dark tones of The Tyrant, but the fact that she was thousands of light years from The Dread Lord emboldened her. "If you hadn't sent the others…"

"Never question my decisions!" The voice was quiet, but nonetheless threatening. "Or you will be truly sorry…"

Tingkat bit her forked tongue and remained silent.

"I have news for you. I have been monitoring teleportation events in your sector. A t-mail sent from your current position has arrived at a location nearby. You must go there immediately. Seize The Server. And this time do not fail."

Tingkat's pulse raced. "Where is it?"

The Tyrant's voice was full of menace "A place called Stonehenge…"

Stonehenge, Salisbury Plain, England

The great stones of Stonehenge were silhouetted against the setting sun. The site was deserted, except for the companions who stood alone in the middle of the ruined circle of stones.

"Strange that our journey should begin here," said Bitz, "considering this was where me and Janus arrived on Earth." He looked up at Jack, who had said nothing since their arrival. "Hey, Jack! You paying attention?"

Jack shook his head slowly. "I was just thinking about how my dad stood up to that crazy alien? I never knew he had it in him."

"Jumping June-bugs! Snap out of it!" yapped Bitz. "We have to find the symbols to activate this site, and then teleport to the next one."

Jack nodded and held out The Server. "Janus said we should ask Help."

Ching! The hologram appeared. *"Have all those alien headbangers gone?"* he asked, taking in the landscape. He did a double take. *"Oh no! We're not here again!"*

"Yes they have," said Bitz. "And yes, we are."

"So what's cooking?"

Jack quickly explained the problem. "Janus said you would have something on Ancient Sites in your data banks."

Help looked pained. *"Something? Something? I have more knowledge in my least important processor than whole planetary systems put together, and you thought I might have something in my databanks. Sheesh!"*

"Then you can tell us how this site should be activated?"

"Work, work, work, work, work," moaned Help. *"How you monkeys ever became self-sufficient, I'll never know."*

"Look it up in your databanks," Merle said sweetly.

"Oh, so suddenly everyone's an advisor," replied Help. It briefly disappeared back into The Server, before re-emerging with a smile on its hologrammatic face. *"OK, here's something I know. When the sun sets or rises, its light reveals symbols on the stones. Push the right one, and 'Hey press-to!' (That's a gag, if anyone's listening...) you activate the site."*

Loaf gave a disparaging snort. "Oh come on! That sort of stuff is so Hollywood. You're joking us, right?"

Help materialized itself a big cigar and a boot-polish

moustache. *"I say, I say, I say what's the difference between an amoeba and the monkey who made that last comment? The amoeba has got more brains!"* The hologram glared at Loaf. "That *was a joke – the information I gave you wasn't."* Help disappeared back into The Server, with a shirty *ching!*

"Nice going, Loaf," said Merle. "Upsetting our information source."

"But that's crazy!" protested Loaf. "You have to wait for the sun to rise or set? What if it was raining?"

"That's the problem with these low-tech sites," said Bitz. "Unreliable."

"Luckily, the sun hasn't set yet," said Jack. "Let's spread out and keep our eyes peeled for any symbols."

As the sun continued its slow descent, the group fanned out across the circle, searching for the signs that would help them to activate the site. The sun dipped lower and lower in the sky. Stonehenge was bathed in the embers of the dying day, but there was nothing to be found.

Finally the sun disappeared from the evening sky and darkness enveloped the ancient monument.

The companions gathered together by one of the great stones.

Loaf gave a shrug. "So the Hollywood bit didn't work. What do we do now?"

Jack shook his head. "I don't know."

USAF Base, Little Slaughter, near Cambridge, England

"Have we managed to re-establish contact with the outside world?" asked Colonel Stone.

Major Jackson shook his head. "Still complete communication blackout. No one knows what's been happening here."

Colonel Stone grimaced. "Let me know as soon as we have a phone working. I have to contact Merle."

It had been a heck of a few days. His daughter had gone missing, then turned up again with some crazy story about aliens that he didn't believe for one minute, until things with tentacles and more than the regulation number of heads had started appearing like wasps round a picnic. Then Merle and her friends had disappeared before his very eyes, and to top it all, there were a couple of dead aliens in his ops room. *The X Files* had nothing on this – how was it all going to sound in a report?

"The base is clear," replied the major. "The bug-eyed monsters seem to have disappeared. We have the situation under control."

"You think so?" Frank Stone's voice was bitter. "My kid's out there, Hal. Facing the Lord knows what."

"Colonel." The voice at his shoulder was that of Bill Armstrong. "She's with my lad. He's got his head screwed on, has our Jack." He gave a slight nod. "I'll take my wife home now, if you don't mind. You'll let us know if you hear anything?" Colonel Stone nodded.

Luckily for his peace of mind, he wasn't to know that the invaders had abandoned their attack because they had seen Tingkat leaving the base in pursuit of Merle and her friends. Among the Galaxy's bounty hunters Tingkat had a reputation for finding her prey, so the surviving hunters were pursuing her in space ships, fly-cycles, jet-packs and anything else they could get hold of that would allow them to move at speed.

"Major – get me reports on how many of our birds are down and an update on the state of our missile defence capabilities," Colonel Stone ordered. He stared down at the bodies of Mad Moxie and The Thing with No Name. "And Hal, get those two creatures out of my Ops room."

"Master Sergeant Gelt volunteered to do it. He's on the case as we speak."

"You mean he's gonna try and sell 'em to some film director!" Colonel Stone gave a bark of savage laughter, not knowing how near the truth he was. "Keep the base on a state of Red Alert. If any more of those alien creatures appear, give it to 'em good."

Unfortunately for Tracer and Zodiac Hobo, the next alien ship to appear over the air force base was Trigger.

Zodiac was still shaking from the encounter with the worm hole. "They were all wormy, man. Wriggly with teeth! I've not had a trip like that since I mistook some Andalesian Funny Juice for a glass of water!"

"Please be quiet, Mr Hobo, I'm trying to concentrate," said Tracer, poring over Trigger's sensors. "Hmm. There are indications that alien vessels have arrived at the air base. I wonder what's been going on?"

Zodiac brightened. "Hey, if they've been making, like, First Contact – maybe the humans will be cool and put out a welcoming party for us."

He was partly right. The air base had laid on a party, but not the welcoming sort.

WHHHHHOOOOSSHHHH!

BANG!

A surface-to-air missile skimmed across Trigger's port side and exploded.

"Ow!" moaned the ship. *"That hurt!"*

Another missile exploded in front of Trigger. The ship shook violently from side to side.

"I hate bangs!" moaned Zodiac. "They're noisy and lead to blood and stuff like that." He buried his head in his hands. "Oh dude, what a bummer!"

Three F15 fighters appeared from behind Trigger, cannons blazing.

"Helppppppp!" screamed Trigger. *"What have I done to them? Why are they shooting at me? Nobody likes me. I should never have left my systems programmer..."*

"Ship!" snapped Tracer. "I urgently suggest you take avoiding action."

"I can't!" sobbed Trigger. *"I'm just useless!"*

"Just take us straight up, you idiot machine!" howled Tracer. "Whoosh Factor Six."

"Ooooh!" said Trigger wonderingly. *"I never thought of that."*

The F15 pilots gasped in amazement as the space ship they had plumb in their sights disappeared in the blink of an eye.

Back on board Trigger, Tracer gave a sigh of relief. "Why do I have to do all the thinking on this ship?" He gave Zodiac a hard look. "Oh, yes. Now I remember." He drummed eighteen claws on the scanner console. "I wonder where those humans can be hiding?"

Stonehenge, Salisbury Plain, England

"So what do we do now?" asked Loaf, glumly. "Sit here?"

"Not a good idea," said Googie. "The hunters will soon pick up our trail. They could be here any minute."

"We need to ask Help." Jack set The Server down on one of the fallen stones and waited. The hologram showed no signs of appearing.

"Help?" repeated Jack. "Can you come out?"

A note flashed up on the screen:

*not uNtil thE pRimAte saYs
He's sOrry.*

"Say sorry, Loaf," said Jack.

"Why?" moaned Loaf.

"Do it!" they all shouted.

Loaf sighed. "All right. All right. Sorry," he mumbled

i cAn't hEar you.

"Sorry."

louder!

"SORRY!" screamed Loaf.

Ching! Help shot out. *"If love is never having to say you're sorry,"* he said. *"You can safely assume that we ain't ever gonna tie the knot."*

Loaf gave a low snarl.

"So whadda ya want now, primates?"

Jack pointed at the stones. "We couldn't find the symbols."

"Of course you couldn't," replied Help matter-of-factly. *"These stones have been around over three thousand years – the markings have obviously worn off in that time."*

"Why ... didn't ... you ... tell ... us?" demanded Merle, slowly.

"You ... didn't ... ask ... me," answered Help. *"You said, 'How should the site be activated', and I told you. What you should have asked was, 'How can we activate*

the site?' That's the trouble with you semi-evolved life forms, muddled thinking..."

Jack held up his hand. "We haven't got time for this. What do we do?"

The hologram suddenly became helpful. "There's probably still some residual markings left on the stones, but you'd only be able to see them in ultra-red light."

Jack looked puzzled. "Ultra-red? I've heard of ultra-violet and infra-red light, I've never heard of ultra-red."

Help's head bobbed from side-to-side. "That's because you monkeys haven't discovered it yet. You have to have discovered hyper-drive technology before you discover ultra-red."

Googie and Bitz nodded. "He's right."

"Ultra-red will pick out the symbols, no problem." The hologram materialized itself a pair of snazzy sunglasses and stripes of sun-block appeared across its nose and cheeks. "Lighten up, people."

The monument was bathed in a strange purple-red glow. The stones shimmered as their secret was revealed. Every stone was covered in elaborate symbols – geometric shapes and leaf-patterns with, running through them, an elaborate pattern of vertical scratches. These were set in complex groupings above, below and cutting through horizontal straight lines, which stood out against the grey of the rock.

Jack studied the patterns. "Celtic knots," he said. "But I

don't know what those scratches are."

"*Primitive writing,*" drawled Help. "*I'll have to decode it. Childishly simple, of course, for an Artificial Intelligence with my processing capacity…*"

"Then you'd better get on with it." Merle's voice was tense. "We have company."

With a blast of sound, the horseshoe-shaped craft Merle had seen earlier ripped through the sky overhead at several times the speed of sound. As the companions watched, the vessel slowed and began to turn back towards them.

Loaf groaned. "Help! Get the lead out, willya?"

"*I'm working on it, Primate. Don't rush me.*" Help hummed to itself.

Merle's phone rang. She gave Jack an incredulous glance as she hauled it out of her pocket. "If this is some dumb telesales call…" She flipped it open. "Hello? *Dad?* Yeah, I'm fine…" She eyed the approaching hunter's craft and added, "…ish. You got the phones working? That's neat. I'm at Stonehenge…" Merle dived for cover as an energy weapon cut a broad swathe through the grass towards her and hit a fallen stone, which shattered. "Listen, I can't talk right now, we're being shot at by an alien spaceship … catch you later."

The ship was turning for another pass. At the same time, three more vessels appeared, coming in from varying points of the compass.

"That's it!" Suddenly the ultra-red light Help was producing focused on two lines of script, lying above and below a single Celtic knot. *"I got a translation. This is what it says…"*

Words appeared on the screen behind Help:

Touch here
and stand well back.

Help beamed. *"I'm so brilliant, sometimes I even surprise myself."*

Without replying, Jack hurled himself at the illuminated symbol, and pressed it.

A faint roar sounded deep within the stone, then gave out. Jack pressed again, harder this time. There was a series of chugs, sounding like a car starting up after a long night in the rain. The stones began to hum. The sound built rapidly in pitch. The air around Jack and the others crackled and buzzed. As the four alien ships converged on the ancient ruin, lines of discharged force shot between the stones, building to a whirlpool of blue-white light.

Tingkat Bumbag, distracted by the light show below, flew her ship straight into one of the other converging vessels. The glancing blow sent her spinning crazily out of control. Her crippled machine ploughed into the ground. Simultaneously, the other two bounty hunters' ships smashed into each other head on, and vaporized instantly.

Crawling from her wrecked ship (Tingkat's species were notoriously tough), the bounty hunter watched stony-faced as the whirlpool of energy which spun inside the stones enveloped the companions. In the blink of an eye, her prey disappeared.

5

The Pyramids, near Cairo, Egypt

Jack, Merle and Loaf found themselves sitting on some kind of stone or concrete bench. Although the sky was completely dark, the air was very warm. Googie was on Merle's lap, and Jack felt Bitz's hairy body pressed against his shins. All around them, people were staring at them and chattering excitedly in several different languages – probably discussing their unconventional arrival. Jack hurriedly slammed The Server's lid shut on Help.

"Hey!" protested the Hologram in muffled tones, *"Who turned the lights out?!"*

It was an apt comment. The floodlights over their seats dimmed and the voices of the crowd died away. Jack whispered to Merle, "Where are we?"

"TAN-TON-TAAAAAAAA!"

A deafening blast of stirring music slammed the companions back into their seats.

"EGYPT," intoned a booming, amplified voice. "LAND OF THE PHARAOHS, WHERE THE BARREN DESERT IS WASHED BY THE FERTILE WATERS OF THE RIVER NILE..."

Spotlights pierced the darkness. Slightly to their right loomed an enormous stone head: a human face with its nose and part of its upper lip missing, framed by a formal headdress. More lights revealed that the head rested on the gigantic body of a lion.

"HERE, THE MAJESTIC SPHINX STANDS ETERNAL GUARD OVER THE CITY OF THE DEAD…"

Another sequence of lights revealed a triangular-shaped mountain of rock, right in front of them. Loaf clicked his fingers excitedly. "I know where we are! We're at the Pyramids."

Merle gave him a scornful look. "Did you work that out all by yourself?"

"THIS IS THE GREAT PYRAMID OF KHUFU," the voice declaimed, "KNOWN TO THE GREEKS AS CHEOPS…"

The lights on the pyramid dimmed: laser beams speared out to form an image of the Pharaoh on the side of the Great Pyramid.

Bitz clambered on to Jack's lap and gazed at the light show. "What's happening?"

"Shhhh!" Jack cast nervous glances at the surrounding seats, where people were starting to point at Bitz and nudge each other. "You're a dog, remember?"

"HERE, THE PHARAOH BEGINS HIS JOURNEY TO THE AFTERLIFE, WHILE HIS MORTAL REMAINS ARE GUARDED BY ANUBIS, THE JACKAL-HEADED GOD, AND BASTET, DAUGHTER OF THE SUN-GOD RE…"

The lasers projected the image of a cat-headed goddess. Googie purred approval. "Say what you like about the Ancient Egyptians, they sure knew how to treat cats."

"OK," whispered Merle, "so we're at the Pyramids. Does anybody know what we have to do here?"

"This is the second Ancient Site," said Googie in a stage whisper. "We have to activate its defensive function, and teleport on to the third."

Merle stared at the cat. "And where do we have to be to do that?"

Googie indicated the Great Pyramid with a languid paw. "At a guess – in there."

Loaf's jaw dropped. "Mummy!"

Merle stared at him. "You want your mom? How old are you?"

"I mean, there could be a mummy in there!" Loaf's eyes were wide and frightened. "A horrible Egyptian mummy, all bandages and bad news, and if we go disturbing it, it'll curse us and we'll get eaten by beetles and…"

"Ssssh!" A lady sitting behind Loaf flapped at him with her programme.

Jack gripped Loaf's arm tightly. "Shut up. We can't do anything now, there are too many people around." He indicated a number of white-uniformed guards patrolling the fringes of the crowd. "We'll have to sneak out later. Just sit back and enjoy the show."

"MANY TALES ARE TOLD," boomed the recorded voice cheerfully, "OF THE DREADFUL FATE OF THOSE WHO TRIED TO STEAL FROM THE PHAROAH'S TOMB..."

"Enjoy the show," said Loaf faintly. "Yeah, right."

Stonehenge, Salisbury Plain, England

The bounty hunter from the planet Anubia who had collided with Tingkat had fared rather better than she had. His ship was almost intact. He had landed, and completed a hurried survey of the Stonehenge site. The Server was not there – he had hardly expected it to be. The Anubian was about to climb into his craft when he stiffened. The muzzle of a laser-pistol was tickling the hair behind his ear.

The owner of the pistol said, "I need your ship."

Having no sweat-glands, the dog-headed Anubian lolled his tongue out and panted nervously. "Tingkat! How're you doing?"

"Not too good," said Tingkat regretfully. "You totalled my ship. That's why I'm taking yours."

The Anubian nodded – very carefully. "Fine – but you'll need me as well."

"I think not."

"I think so. You want to know where our prey has gone?"

The pressure on the Anubian's neck eased very slightly. "Surely," Tingkat said softly, "you weren't thinking of keeping information about the humans' whereabouts to yourself?" She clicked her tongue. "Shame on you."

"My species knows of another Ancient Site." The Anubian licked its lips nervously.

"Keep talking."

"We built it ourselves, on one of the other continents of this world. The people who lived there worshipped my species as gods."

"That shows a certain lack of discrimination," sneered Tingkat.

"My guess is that the humans and their allies have gone there. I can…" The creature gasped as the pistol was jammed into its neck. "I mean, *we* can be there in a few gala-minutes. "

Tingkat nodded. "Makes sense. Here's the deal. You fly me to this place, and I'll take The Server."

"And what's in it for me?" demanded the Anubian.

"Your life."

The Anubian swallowed hard. "That seems fair…"

Moments after the Anubian ship had blasted off, Trigger arrived. The battered ship wobbled as Zodiac's inexpert piloting took it on a sweep of the stone circle. It hovered for a while over Tingkat's crashed vessel.

Tracer peered down at the wreck and ground his needle-sharp teeth. "It seems we're too late. I suppose we'd better land and see if we can pick up any clues as to where the humans have gone."

"No need, dude." Zodiac pointed at a complex pattern of loops and circles that had been crushed and burnt into the grass of an adjoining field. "Crop circle. Check it out. Looks to me like the landing marks of an Anubian ship."

Tracer mused. "If you're right – that does happen sometimes, I suppose?"

"Hey!"

Tracer nodded. "Then there is only one place they can have gone."

Seconds later, Zodiac's battered ship lurched into motion, and climbed falteringly into the night sky.

The Pyramids, near Cairo, Egypt

"...AND SO THE PHAROAHS SLEEP UNDER THE WATCH-FUL EYES OF THE SPHINX WHILE THE CENTURIES ROLL BY, THEIR PASSING MARKED ONLY BY THE RESTLESS HEARTBEAT OF THE MAJESTIC NILE."

With blaring brass fanfares and a soaring, wordless chorus, the music ended and the lights dimmed.

Merle's eyes sparkled. "Hey, that was really interesting."

Loaf wriggled in his seat. "I prefer more action. And popcorn."

"You want action?" said Jack in a strained voice. "I think you're about to get it." He pointed.

As the lights of the show faded, a moving speck of brilliance appeared over the shoulder of the Great Pyramid, approaching very fast from the north-west. At first it was silent: then a high-pitched whine made itself heard.

A second later, something big and silver swooped past the Great Pyramid and rocketed over the heads of the audience. The thunderous howl of its passage pounded the eardrums of the crowd. Sand and waste paper was kicked up, making the air gritty. People shrieked, jabbered and pointed. Many remained seated, not sure whether this was supposed to be part of the show.

Jack was under no such illusions. "Bounty hunters. They've found us."

The Anubian studied his sensors as his ship turned to make another pass. "I can't locate them. There are too many people."

Tingkat nodded. "Then lose the people. Didn't you say something about a guardian...?"

The Anubian drew back its dog-like lips in what might have been a smile – or a snarl. "My people left an android life form to guard the tombs. That was a long time ago, of course..."

Tingkat's eyes shone with unholy glee. "Let's see if it still works, shall we?"

The Anubian tapped a series of command codes into his ship's communications console...

...and down below, in the Ancient Site at the edge of the desert, the strange composite creature known as the Sphinx stretched – and stood.

Its stone outer casing cracked, crumbled and fell away. The ancient cyber-beast shrugged off the remains of its body-shaped coffin, and stared around with gleaming, predatory eyes.

Below it and to one side, hundreds of humanoids were running about in all directions making shrill squealing noises. The Sphinx lashed its tail and hissed at them. The squeals got louder.

But five figures – three humanoids and two smaller quadrupeds – had detached themselves from the rest, and were running full-pelt across the desert, making for the largest of the pyramids that the Sphinx had guarded for so long.

The creature gave a yowl of rage that shook windows ten kilometres away and plunged in pursuit.

Merle's phone rang as she ran. She hauled it from her jacket pocket and pressed the "receive" key.

"Hi, Dad … look, this isn't a great time right now…" Merle ran with both hands clasped to her head, one holding her phone, the other pressed against her ear so she could hear her father's distant voice against the infuriated roars of the pursuing creature. "Yeah, we got away, but they caught up with us again … we're being chased by the Sphinx … the Sphinx … S-p-h-i-n-x … you know, seventy metres long, weighs about a million kilos,

woman's head, lion's body … yeah! Hang on, I'm gonna
lose you, we're going into a pyramid … *py-ra-mid* …
oh, nuts!"

She flipped the phone closed and dodged to the side
as the Sphinx pounced. In spite of its cat-like agility, the
android guardian was too massive to turn quickly. By
the time it had changed direction, Merle was panting up
the steps to the narrow entrance to the Great Pyramid.
She joined the others in a narrow passage. From outside,
the Sphinx's yowls of frustration dislodged fragments of
stone from the ceiling. Merle held out the phone. "I knew
bringing this thing was a bad idea … now what?"

Jack rattled a barred steel door. "It's locked. We can't
get in."

"Amateurs." Though Loaf was winded by the long run
through soft sand, he wasn't too exhausted to pass up an
opportunity to be the centre of attention. "Step … aside."
He drew a piece of bent wire from his key-case, and set
to work on the lock. Seconds later he was rewarded by a
sharp click, and the door swung open. Loaf stepped aside.
"Ta-daaa!"

From outside came a ringing command. The Sphinx
hissed. Jack peered out, and grabbed Loaf's arm with
renewed urgency. "Come on!"

"What's your hurry?" protested Loaf. "That thing is
mean, but it's way too big to get in here."

"It's got back-up," Jack reported. "The woman who

nearly caught us in Ops, and some guy with a dog's head, and they aren't."

"Aren't what?"

"Too big to get in here. Come *on!*"

The first corridor led downwards. After stumbling in the dark for several seconds, Jack flipped open The Server. "Help!"

The hologram appeared. *"Hey, primate! Where are we now? It's as dark as a tomb in here!"*

"Well spotted," said Jack tightly. "How about some light?"

"For you, anything," sneered Help: but it closed its eyes and blew out its hologrammatic cheeks as if con-centrating, and its head began to glow with the radiance of a low-powered light bulb.

The companions found themselves standing at the junction of two corridors. One continued to descend; the other climbed away into darkness.

"Down," said Jack, "or up?"

"Up," grunted Loaf, repressing a shudder.

Jack shrugged and started to climb. At first the pas-sageway was narrow and very low, but after they passed another junction the passage opened out and the roof soared to over four times human height. Spurred on by noises from the passage below, the companions clam-bered up the forty-five degree slope with all the speed they could muster.

At length they arrived, gasping, in a chamber large enough to house a double-decker bus. A huge lidless sarcophagus lay to one side of the chamber. Loaf drew back from it. Merle hoisted herself up and peered inside.

"Relax," she told Loaf cheerfully. "Nobody home."

Jack stared round at the featureless walls. "There's nothing here!"

"Hey, Help!" snapped Bitz. "You want to make with the ultra-red again?"

"Work, work, work!" grumbled Help, but it materialized a set of sunglasses and bathed the room with the red-purple colour the companions had first seen at Stonehenge. Almost immediately, glowing patterns began to emerge on the walls of the chamber: bewildering rows of objects, people and animals...

"Hieroglyphics," said Merle. "I did a school project on these." She picked up Googie, who for once made no protest: the cat wanted to see the picture-writing close up.

"C'mon, Help!" snapped Bitz. "Which one do we press?"

"Give me time, willya?" demanded Help. *"Now, lemme see – accessing Rosetta Stone files – if the mouth shape is the sound 'r' and the owl means 'he', then ... got it,"* snapped Help. *"Press that symbol."* The ultra-red light focused on a beautifully detailed carving of a human eye.

Merle gasped. "The Eye of Horus," she breathed. "The

symbol of protection against evil – I should have guessed."

"But you didn't. And now, time's up!" The new voice came from the entrance to the chamber.

Jack turned slowly. The bounty hunter who called herself Tingkat Bumbag was standing behind him, alongside a human figure with the head of a dog … or a jackal.

Tingkat levelled an energy weapon at the companions. "Give me The Server."

Seeing Tingkat's companion, Merle wondered whether she'd been wise to make light of ancient superstition. "Anubis," she breathed. "The jackal-headed god … guardian of the dead."

But the alien's mouth was also open, and he was staring in utmost horror at the small creature in Merle's arms.

"Bastet," he whined. "My ancient enemy … the terror of my people!"

Remembering the commentary at the light show, Merle caught on. She held Googie up. "He thinks you're a rival god," she whispered in the cat's ear. "He's good and spooked. Go get him."

With a "meow" of acknowledgement, Googie leaped lightly from Merle's arms and stalked towards the quaking Anubian. The jackal-headed creature gave a strangled howl of fear, and turned to run: colliding as he did so with Tingkat. The two bounty hunters went down in a heap.

"Go, Googie!" Merle whooped. "Ol' Bastet must have been hot stuff!"

Jack dived for the eye symbol and pressed it, just as Tingkat thrust aside the gibbering Anubian and snatched at her weapon. Too late. Jack, his companions and The Server were bathed in blue-white light. Their bodies dissolved into a dense cloud of particles that flew around the chamber, bouncing off all four walls, before disappearing with a faint whooshing noise up a barely-visible shaft set high in one of its walls.

Tingkat lowered her weapon, and gave the shaking Anubian a furious glare. "Fool!" she spat. "You have robbed me of my opportunity." Her mouth twisted. "I wonder what would have happened if they'd pressed the wrong symbol?"

Tingkat's arm lashed out to press a snake carving. For a moment, nothing happened. Then, with a grinding roar, the solid floor in front of the fading inscriptions parted and swung downwards. A leopard-like leap carried Tingkat to safety: her companion, less agile, disappeared into the blackness below with an inhuman shriek.

Tingkat stared into the void for a moment. She whispered, "Fascinating."

She turned on her heel and left the chamber.

The Anubian lay on his back, every limb aching, and groaned. After a while, he dragged himself on to one elbow, fumbled a small plasma-torch from his belt, switched it on and looked around.

He gave a low whine of terror. He was in a tiny chamber, surrounded by cats. Cat-statues lined the walls, gazing aloofly down at their ancient foe. The bundles occupying the spaces between the statues could only be mummified cats. The Anubian whimpered.

Shortly afterwards, the breath choked in his throat. There were rustlings in the darkness. Some of the band-aged forms seemed to have developed eyes.

The cat-mummies were coming to life.

6

The companions emerged in a stone-walled room. Dim light seeped in through the doorway behind them.

Loaf sighed. "Why can't we ever land up in a hamburger joint?"

There was a loud hiss, and something long, wriggly and scaly scuttled between Loaf's legs. He leaped into the air and gave a falsetto scream. Then he threw himself back against the wall and clutched at his heart. "What ... what ... what...?"

"Looked like an iguana," said Merle offhandedly. "That would put us somewhere in the Americas."

"Well, thank you, Doctor Dolittle," snarled Loaf. "While you're playing 'I-Spy' with the local wildlife, I'm having a major coronary episode here. I thought we'd stumbled into another low-life alien."

Merle shook her head. "Nope. That was one of our genuine home-grown monsters. I wonder where we are now?"

Bitz trotted towards the barely visible doorway

through which the lizard had escaped. "Let's go and find out."

They stepped out from a round building with a conical stone roof, set on a square plinth. Jack blinked in the sudden light. The sun was high in a sky dotted with fleecy white clouds. It was warm, and more humid than their last stopover in Egypt.

Jack, Merle, Loaf, Bitz and Googie looked round. They were in a ruined city. Time-worn buildings in grey stone rose from a grass-covered open space surrounded by trees. Everywhere, brightly dressed tourists strolled about, took photographs or scampered in the wake of bustling guides who carried sticks topped with flags or streamers.

"Popular spot," drawled Loaf. "What say we see if we can find an English-speaking guide and tag along? Find out where this place is?"

"No need." Merle's voice was strange. Jack looked at her quickly. "I know where we are," Merle continued. "Dad brought us here when we were stationed at Edwards – me and Mom – just before she – died." The hesitation was slight. Merle gave Jack a quick "it's OK" smile. She gestured at the majestic ruins. "We're in Mexico. This is Chichén Itzá." She scowled at Loaf. "Before you ask, that isn't some kind of fast food. This is one of the great cities of the Mayans."

Loaf spread his hands. "I wasn't going to say nothin'!"

Merle gestured to the building behind them. "We

arrived in the Caracol. It's supposed to be some kind of stone-age observatory, I think." She pointed to a tiered building flanked by a forest of ramrod-straight columns that marched like a stone army into the jungle behind it. "That's the Temple of the Warriors, and over there is the ball-court."

Loaf whistled. "These guys played football? Wild!"

"Not American football, you bonehead." Merle gave Loaf a disgusted look. "A ball game wasn't just a sporting event for the Mayans. It was a ritual. It was where men played hardball with the gods. It was *sacred*."

Loaf puffed out his chest, showing off his New York Giants shirt. "Well, excuuuse me! Are you implying that NFL *isn't*?"

Merle rolled her eyes and pointed to the highest building in the complex. It rose majestically above the other ruins. Its four, stepped, triangular sides were bisected by towering stone stairways. A squat temple with a dark, pillared doorway in each of its four walls sat brooding on its flattened top.

"And that," said Merle, "is El Castillo."

Loaf gave a hollow groan. "Oh, no! Not *more* pyramids."

The Pyramids, near Cairo, Egypt

Tracer, wearing a robe that concealed his non-human shape from casual observers, regarded the collapsed

Sphinx, and tried to ignore the hawker who kept trying to sell him things. The gigantic android had expired with the departure of the Anubian ship. Now it lay motionless, surrounded by curious Egyptians, stunned guards and tourists who were clearly trying to cope with far more culture shock than they'd bargained for.

The hawker waved a strip of brightly coloured pictures in front of Tracer's face. "My friend! You want to buy postcards?" Tracer shook his head, grimly regretting the almost universal command of languages that went with his former job and allowed him to understand the man's sledgehammer sales pitch. "Mineral water? Very good, very cold, very … wet?" Tracer irritably waved him away.

Zodiac ambled over. "Hey, man, ask him if he saw the kids."

Tracer sighed, but put the question to the hawker, who nodded eagerly. "Oh, yes, my friend. Just now, I saw the god Anubis go into the pyramid, following three young tourists and a dog and a cat – and…" He paused significantly. "…And a strange-looking woman with green hair and green skin."

Tracer hissed through his teeth. "Tingkat Bumbag! The most ruthless bounty hunter of them all."

Zodiac raised his eyebrows. "Yeah? Sounds like a real hot babe."

Tracer turned back to the hawker. "Did they all come back out again?"

The man shook his head. "Oh, no. Only the strange woman came out."

"Then we are too late." Tracer stormed off towards the dark corner where they had parked *Trigger*. Zodiac had to run to keep up. "Tingkat must have double-crossed the Anubian and stolen his ship," Tracer announced after some thought. "The pyramid is armed – your instruments picked that up when we were still over a thousand kilometres away – so Jack Armstrong and his friends have been here, and if they did not leave the pyramid, they must have teleported to their next destination."

As they approached Zodiac's ship, a nightmarish howl of fear and agony rose from the depths of the Great Pyramid and echoed across the desert. Zodiac shivered. "Hey, man, like, what was that?"

"The Anubian finding his way into the Afterlife," said Tracer without breaking stride, "if I'm any judge."

"Whooo. Sounds like a real drag." Zodiac followed Tracer through Trigger's main hatchway, nodding intelligently. "So, like – what *is* the next destination?"

Tracer logged on to the Outernet. His nimble fingers flew over the touch-sensitive keys of Trigger's main computer console. "Another Ancient Site – perhaps another pyramid on another continent." Images appeared on the screen. Tracer nodded grimly. "There are several possibilities. We have some searching to do."

Zodiac nodded. "OK, dude, you got it. Do we have time

to call in for pizza?" Tracer shook his head. "Drive-thru?"

"No."

Zodiac slumped in the pilot's seat. "Slave-driver."

Trigger rose erratically into the sky, and headed into the west.

Chichén Itzá, Mexico

The companions had climbed the steep steps to the top of El Castillo. Loaf had complained every step of the way. Then, when they'd entered the pyramid-top temple, they'd had to wait until it was clear of tourists. That had taken a long time.

Now, finally, they were alone. Jack opened The Server. "Help."

The hologram popped into view. *"Oh, mercy!"* said Help sarcastically. *"Another cheery location. Have you monkeys ever thought of taking some time on the beach? Or maybe going into the home improvement business?"*

"Less lip," Merle told it firmly, "and more ultra-red."

Help scowled. *"I was just trying to lighten the atmosphere. No need to get tetchy."* But its sunglasses reappeared: the chamber flooded with the strange light, and once more patterns began to form.

"Mayan glyphs," said Merle authoritatively. Loaf stared at her. Merle shrugged. "I don't know much about them except they're a kind of picture-writing, like Egyptian hieroglyphics. Each of those little square pictures is a word. It's a pretty tough language – it took the experts years to decipher."

Loaf nodded wisely. "So we need Help to figure out the instructions to activate the site and t-mail us to the next one."

Help groaned. *"Oh, my aching processors! OK, OK."* The grouchy hologram materialized itself a deerstalker hat, a droopy pipe and an outsized magnifying glass with which it examined the Mayan symbols. *"Got it! Elementary, my dear primates."* Once more, the light beam focused on a single pattern of symbols. *"Press that symbol there."* Confidently, Loaf did so.

Nothing happened.

A worried look crossed Help's face. *"Or maybe it should have been* that *one over* there..."

Without warning, the floor beneath them gave way. Yelling (and barking and meowing) with fright, the companions fell.

They tumbled into darkness, sliding down what seemed to be an enormously long chute. Wisps of stringy material brushed their faces as they fell. (Jack thought about giant spider webs and hoped these were vines).

After a descent, which lasted several heart-stopping seconds, they tumbled into soft sand. More shocked than hurt, they picked themselves up.

"Is everyone OK?" asked Merle.

Googie hissed. "That was *so* undignified – and I

think I broke a claw."

"Is that all?" Loaf rubbed his backside and winced. "Lucky you. He rounded on their hologrammatic help-mate. "Wait until I get my hands on you," he growled.

"*Whoops!*" Help turned pale. "*The management cannot be held responsible for anything at all. The value of your investments may go down as well as up. Absolutely no guarantees, exchanges, refunds or credit notes will be given.*" It blew Loaf a kiss, and vanished.

Jack picked up The Server and looked around. "Wow," he said.

They stood in a cavern of enormous proportions. Huge stalactites, metres long, hung glistening from the roof, which soared above them, the height of a cathedral nave. Sunlight poured through a single hole amidst the petrified stone icicles, and shone on a deep blue underground lake.

Merle moved to Jack's side. "They call these places 'cenotés'. Some of them are open to tourists, but I never saw one this big. I guess maybe nobody's discovered it yet."

"Nobody human, to be precise," said a strange, hissing voice from somewhere behind them.

"Loaf," said Merle without turning round, "who just said that?"

"I don't know," said Loaf in a far-off voice. "What would you call a gigantic snake with feathers and wings?"

Merle remained rooted to the spot. "I'm not sure," she said faintly. "A winged serpent, I guess."

"Oh. Well, there's a winged serpent behind you."

Merle and Jack turned round and gazed open-mouthed at the strange creature that reared up halfway to the cavern roof, maintaining its balance with unhurried beats of its great wings. "Quetzalcoatl," breathed Merle.

The creature blinked in the disconcerting way that snakes do. "Quet-zal-co-atl," it said slowly. "Yes, that was one of my many names. I was also known as Ku-kul-can by the people of the city above – many years ago." It gave a rather sad little sigh.

Merle found herself at a loss. "Are you a god?" she asked.

The creature put its snake-head on one side. "No – at least, I don't think so. Though I've often been mistaken for one. I've been here an awfully long time, you see."

"How long?" demanded Bitz bluntly.

"Well, let me think now." Quetzalcoatl mused. "Around four thousand Earth years or so." It ignored the companions' gasps and exclamations. "Yes, quite that, I think. It's fortunate that I am of a long-lived species. It's been such a long task, you see."

Jack caught on. "So – you're an alien."

"Oh, I'm not native to earth." The gigantic creature giggled. "Obviously."

"You mentioned a task," said Bitz. "What task?"

"My project." The winged snake drew itself up proudly, until its head nearly disappeared among the stalactites high above. "I am a scientist. My species gave me a grant to pursue a project to understand the human race."

Googie gave Quetzalcoatl an inscrutable cat-stare. "And this project of yours has been going on for four thousand *years*?"

The strange being suddenly looked sheepish. "Well," it said in subdued tones, "I didn't *plan* it that way. I was supposed to deliver my report millennia ago. But whenever I thought I'd finished it, humans kept coming up with behaviour I just couldn't believe. So I'd have to study that, of course ... and then, later, they started bringing me tissue samples..."

Googie's eyes narrowed. "Tissue samples?" she repeated.

Quetzalcoatl nodded vigorously. "Oh, yes. Would you like to see them? I keep them in the next cave – cryogenically frozen so they won't decompose. This way."

The next cave was even bigger than the first, though it had no hole in the roof. Every wall was stacked from floor to ceiling with glowing pods.

Jack took a look in one. A warrior in a feathered head-dress lay inside. He had a big hole in his chest. Wordlessly, Jack joined Merle. She was staring in horror at the body of a young woman. She also had a hole in her chest – right above where her heart would be.

Merle spun round with a stifled cry, and pointed a shaking finger at Quetzalcoatl. "Tissue samples?" She choked back a sob of pure horror. "Is that what you call them? These are human sacrifices!"

Quetzalcoatl gave her a haughty stare. "It was not my business to enquire how these samples reached me. I am a scientist. An observer. I am not involved."

Merle gritted her teeth. "Come on," she ordered the companions. "We're leaving."

With a speed amazing for a creature of its bulk, Quetzalcoatl blocked their way. "Oh, I think not," it hissed. There was nothing friendly or vague about the black snake-eyes now. "You see, my people stopped bringing me samples several hundred years ago, and I've finished cataloguing all those I have. I really wouldn't try to escape if I were you," it went on, seeing Loaf edging towards the cave exit. "I assure you, I am extremely venomous." It bared fangs as long and sharp as a cavalry sabre. "I urge cooperation."

There was a sound of thunder. The earth shook. A couple of stalactites fell from the roof of the cave and buried their points in its floor. The companions staggered, and Quetzalcoatl fell flat on its nose. A cloud of dust billowed through the passageway into the first cave.

"My cave," hissed the infuriated serpent. "Someone has discovered my cave!" It folded its wings and shot through the narrow passageway at amazing speed.

Jack looked around. "Quick – while it's gone! That thing must have had a way of bringing the bodies down here."

It was Bitz who found the freight elevator – a plain door of some alien substance moulded to look like stone. The controls were simple. Once they'd piled into the narrow space and the door had shut behind them, a push on a button with an arrow pointing up sent them into an uncomfortably fast ascent.

The companions emerged in the centre of the temple they had so precipitately left only a few minutes ago, giving a group of Italian tourists the shock of their lives. Racing out into the open air, they stood on top of the pyramid and stared in amazement out over the ruins.

Far below, tourists were rushing for shelter, except for a few foolhardy ones who were trying to take pictures. In the skies above, a strange battle was being fought. Tingkat had arrived. Her sensors had located The Server in an underground cavern – but in trying to blast a way through to its location, she had disturbed a large and savage creature that seemed to have taken grave exception to her presence.

Tingkat, in her stolen ship, was trying everything she knew to get Quetzalcoatl in her sights: but the infuriated snake god slid through the air as an eel does through water, and was proving twice as slippery. Bursts of fire and raucous screeches of rage rolled over the ancient stones of the Mayan City.

Merle's phone rang. She flipped it open. "Hi, Dad. Yes, I'm fine, I was just about to be sacrificed to a snake god, but he got called away on business. Where am I? On top of a pyramid … no, not that pyramid, another pyramid … yes, I did say snake-god … it's kinda preoccupied right now, it's having a fight with a spaceship … whoa! That thing is fast! Listen, I'll catch up with you later, OK? We've got things to do. Bye."

Jack led the way back into the temple and called for Help. "Now," he told the hologram, "let's try that again. And no foul-ups this time, OK?"

Help scowled. *"Gee, one little mistake."* It caught the companions' glares. *"OK, OK. It's a tough language, I think one of you mentioned that. Press that picture over there."*

Jack's hand hovered over the glyph. "This one?"

"Yup."

"Sure?"

"Sure, I'm sure."

"You were sure last time."

"Sue me. This time I'm double certain sure."

Dubiously, Jack pressed his hand on the picture. Immediately, the hum they had first heard inside the Great Pyramid sounded from beneath them. A moment later, with a flare of blue-white light, the companions were gone.

Tingkat was finding her opponent too hot to handle. The winged serpent was faster and much more manoeuvrable than the clumsy Anubian ship. A glancing blow sent the bounty hunter slewing through the air, yawing violently. As Tingkat fought desperately for control, Quetzalcoatl, the snake-god, plunged roaring in pursuit, and closed in for the kill.

7

Uluru, Northern Territory, Australia

"That is one heck of a lump of rock!" exclaimed Loaf, craning his neck in a futile attempt to take in the huge sandstone mass that rose up against the dawn sky. "But at least it isn't another pyramid."

Merle checked her phone. "Wherever we are, it's in the middle of nowhere – there's no reception."

"It's Ayers Rock," said Jack. "I've seen pictures. We're in the middle of Australia."

The companions took in their latest surroundings. The rock rose dramatically out of a pancake-flat desert scrubland of sand, grasses and bushes. A heavy smell of eucalyptus hung on the early morning air.

The sun rose, causing the rock to change colour. The monolith slowly transformed from a dull grey into a dark red hue, as if the sun's warming rays were causing blood to pulse through the very rock itself, bringing it to life.

"So why are we here?" asked Merle. "Where's the Ancient Site?"

"I don't know," said Jack. "But we aren't alone."

He pointed to an area not too far away, where groups of tourists were gathered around taking photographs of the sunrise over one of the natural wonders of the world.

Merle gestured at The Server in Jack's hands. "Let's find some place away from the crowds and see if our friendly neighbourhood hologram can tell us where this site is."

The group set off on a track that ran around the base of the rock, which stretched out for several kilometres. Its sandstone walls were scarred with ravines, gullies and small caves. For a while they walked in silence. A couple of small red lizards appeared, scooting from holes and crevices to bathe in the rays of the rising sun.

Suddenly Bitz pricked up his ears. He came to a stop. "Shhh! Listen," he hissed, flattening himself on the ground. Following his example, the others crouched low. There was a low resonant drone coming from one of the small gullies in the rock. It had an unearthly sound.

"A space ship?" wondered Merle.

"Could be a bounty hunter," said Googie, lashing her tail.

"But how could they be here already?" Jack whispered.

The droning noise grew louder. Mixed with the under-lying hum, the companions could make out the cry of animals and the call of birds. Barks, yowls, yelps, squawks, chirps and croaks filled the air. The sound became more urgent.

Jack gave a yell and clicked his fingers. "I know what it is!" he said. Hurrying towards the noise, he beckoned to the others. "Come on." Cautiously, they followed him into the sandstone gully, towards the source of the noise.

At the end of the gully, sitting cross-legged on a ledge, was a white-haired, bearded aborigine. The old man was blowing into a long hollowed-out tree trunk that rested on his bare legs.

"A didgeridoo!" announced Jack. "That's what the sound was."

"It'll never replace music," muttered Loaf.

The aborigine seemed unaware of the companions. He continued to play his ancient instrument. A cacophony of sounds resonated through the morning air.

As he listened to the almost primeval noise, Jack studied the wiry figure before him. He was bare-chested and wore only a few scraps of leather round his waist. Deep lines of experience and knowledge were etched into his dark face. Bushy white eyebrows hid his eyes. Loaf turned to Jack and whispered. "There's something strange about this guy – he's not breathing!"

The man suddenly stopped playing and looked up with a grin. "No, mate. I blow and take in air through my nose at the same time. Circular breathing, see." He blew a few notes to demonstrate.

Loaf raised an eyebrow. "That's some trick! Imagine being able to eat a king-size double cheeseburger without having to breathe between bites." His eyes took on a dreamy, faraway look.

The old man set aside the wooden instrument. "G'day. The name's Albert. I been expecting you."

Jack looked puzzled. "How did you know we were coming?"

In reply, the old man merely smiled. "Uluru is a place where many paths and trails cross."

Loaf glared at Jack. "I thought you said this place was called Ayers Rock."

"That's what the settlers called it," said the old man peaceably. "We aborigines call it Uluru. I reckon your iwara brought you here."

"Our what?" asked Merle.

"Your iwara – your path. Just like my iwara – my ancestor's path – brought me."

"Ohh! You've been teleporting round the planet too?" asked Loaf, sarcastically. Merle gave him a sharp dig with her elbow.

Albert chuckled. "There's more than one way to fly around the planet, mate," he said enigmatically. "Fancy something out my dilly-bag?" He reached into a bark carry-all by his side, pulled out a cloth and unfolded it. It was full of grubs and beetles. "Bush tucker," he explained. "Anyone for breakfast?"

Merle, Jack and Googie all politely declined. Loaf stared at the food in horror. "I'll just take the fries."

Bitz licked his chops. "What's on offer?"

Albert picked up a couple of large white wriggly things and held them before Bitz's nose. "Witchety grubs."

Bitz gulped – and grinned. "Tasty. Keep 'em coming!"

The others watched, squirming, as Bitz and Albert breakfasted. "Do you know why your path has led you here?" asked Albert between wriggly mouthfuls.

"We're using the Ancient Sites to travel," replied Jack. "We have to find the next one."

The aborigine gestured around him "You've found it, mate. The site is Uluru itself."

Loaf curled his lip. "How can a rock be an Ancient Site? It's not as if someone built it."

Albert gave Loaf a pitying stare. It was a look born of the knowledge of thousands of years, passed down from generation to generation. "Sure they did, mate. Uluru was formed in the Dreamtime, the time of creation, when our ancestors sang the people … the land … everything into existence."

Loaf raised a disbelieving eyebrow but said nothing.

"Who are you?" asked Merle.

The old man smiled. "Like I said, the name's Albert. I'm one of the Anangu – the people." He patted at the rock. "You wanted to find the Ancient Site. This is it. And I'm one of its caretakers." He nodded at Jack "Just like you are…" he said, pointing at The Server.

Jack wondered how Albert knew about his task.

"You're not The Weaver, are you?" he asked.

Albert gave a chuckle. "Here, everything is woven together – the land, the law, the people, the creatures." He shook his head. "No, mate. I'm not The Weaver."

"But can you help us?" Merle asked.

Albert considered. When at last he spoke, his voice was solemn. "On Uluru, there are sacred sites where only a chosen few may enter." He stood up. "I reckon you've been chosen. Follow me."

Chichén Itzá, Mexico

Zodiac watched the battle between Tingkat and Quetzalcoatl rage above the jungle. "Looks like the green babe is in trouble."

"Good," said Tracer offhandedly. "Her attacker is an Aspian. I wonder what it's doing on Earth?" He gave a multi-armed shrug. "Well, it's no concern of ours. The creature isn't bothering us. Take us in while it's finishing her off."

"Man, were you always this mean, or did you take evening classes?" Zodiac angled Trigger towards the pyramid far below: immediately attracting Quetzalcoatl's attention.

"*Oh no!*" squealed Trigger. "*It's attacking me, now!*" With a howl of overloaded engines, the overwrought vessel pulled away from the flying serpent's clutches in a tight high-G turn and shot wildly into the sky.

"Turn back and arm your weapons," snarled Tracer. "We'll teach the Aspian some manners."

"Sorry, dude." Zodiac looked sheepish. "No can do. This is a peace-loving, environmentally friendly ship. It don't have no weapons."

Tracer slapped himself on the forehead. Six times. "Of all the millions of space ships in the Galaxy, I end up on this clapped out, impotent pile of junk!"

"You'll be sorry you said that," wailed Trigger.

Tracer turned on Zodiac. "I thought you were supposed to be a space desperado."

Zodiac shrugged. "Dude, I'm desperate most of the time. Mostly, I'm desperate to stay out of trouble!"

The Aspian continued to circle above the pyramid, guarding its lair. Tracer considered the situation for a moment before opening up a communications channel. An image of Tracer's rival appeared on Trigger's viewscreen.

Tracer gave an ironic bow. "Tingkat."

Tingkat's face momentarily betrayed surprise. "Well, well. Tracer. What brings you to this neck of the Galaxy? Don't tell me you're after The Server for yourself?"

Tracer ignored Tingkat's question. "I have a proposal for you to consider."

"Propose away. I'm listening."

"Sensors indicate that this site has been activated, which means our prey is getting away. The longer we wait here, the cooler the trail will be. Therefore, I suggest that my vessel distracts the Aspian, whilst you take the opportunity to ruffle its feathers. In the most literal sense," he added.

Trigger gave a little moan. *"I hate this plan already!"* Zodiac burrowed his head into his hands.

Tingkat raised a green eyebrow. "And then...?"

"And then we meet at the pyramid and continue the hunt."

Tingkat slowly nodded agreement. "I advise you not to double-cross me, or you'll be next on my list."

Tracer looked hurt. "Tingkat – as if I would."

Despite protests from Trigger and Zodiac, Tracer ordered the ship to head for the Aspian. Weeping with terror, Trigger skimmed the creature, buzzing and flitting around it like an annoying mosquito. Quetzalcoatl roared and lashed at the ship with its whip-like tail – until Tingkat came shooting from out of the sun and launched a plasma-bolt attack that sent Quetzalcoatl, keening with shock and pain, plunging back through the entrance to its hidden cave. The battle was over.

Fifteen minutes later, Tracer and Zodiac were standing in the empty chamber at the top of El Castillo.

"Where did the green chick go?" wondered Zodiac

"Mr Hobo, when Tingkat arrives, I suggest that you do not refer to her as 'chick', unless you want to lose several useful parts of your anatomy."

Zodiac gave Tracer a conspiratorial nudge. "Feisty gal, huh? Groovy."

Tracer ignored Zodiac. "Time waits for no being. Let's find out where these humans have taken The Server."

"You can do that?"

Tracer gave Zodiac a contemptuous glare. "During my lifetime, I have traced and monitored billions of communications from the furthest reaches of the Galaxy. This task is small in comparison." He faced the wall and placed his six-clawed hands on the glyphs.

Zodiac looked puzzled. "Hey dude, hugging rocks, that's kinda cosmic, but how's it gonna tell us where to go?"

"I'm feeling for the afterglow." Tracer's visor pulsed red. "Good. It's still here." He concentrated hard. "Another continent. A rock in the middle of a desert ... a place called ... Australia!"

"Australia! Excellent!"

Tracer and Zodiac spun round as one. Tingkat stood in the doorway. Zodiac's knees turned to jelly. The bounty hunter gave an apologetic wave of the hand. "I got lost."

"Lost?" demanded Tracer. "How? To climb a pyramid, you start at the bottom and carry on up to the top. There are not many places you can get side-tracked."

Tingkat ignored the remark. "So it's a race to The Server. May the best being win. Last one to the other side of the planet is a Sirian Slug-sloth." She turned and sprinted out of the chamber.

Zodiac watched her go with a big stupid grin on his face. His eyes were wide open and his tongue hung out "Oh man! What a babe!"

Tracer dragged the drooling space-hippy out of the door and down the pyramid. "She's an ice-cold killing machine, and you're a feckless idiot. It would never work." Tracer increased his pace until they had to run to avoid going down the steps head over heels. "Come on!" hissed Tracer with low cunning. "The quicker we get to the ship, the quicker you get to see her again."

But on reaching Zodiac's ship, they found Trigger in a state of shock.

"*Infamy! Infamy – everyone's got it in for me!*" cried the ship. "*I've been violated!*"

"Tingkat!" Tracer punched at the control panels. They were dead. "She's sabotaged the ship. That's why she was late."

"*She ... she touched my terminals!*" Trigger wept. "*She fried my chips!*"

"Tingkat did this? Oh man, tell me it ain't so!" Zodiac wailed. "I never want to see her shining green face again! What're we gonna do, dude?"

"Initiate repairs. And don't worry." Tracer's visor pulsed brightly. "There's more than one way to catch a Rabbian Sleekit Cowrin' Timrous Beastie. The clever hunter waits for the prey to come to him..."

Uluru, Northern Territory, Australia

The Friends were standing in a small cave. Albert had lit a fire. The orange flames flickered brightly, lighting up the cave walls and revealing strange carvings and paintings. Multicoloured and complex patterns intermingled with the shapes of people, animals and birds.

"They're beautiful," said Merle.

Albert ran a hand across the layers of paint. "They're a connection between the past and present, the people and the land and..." he paused for a second, "...the earthly and unearthly." He turned to Jack. "Reckon you should choose what you need. If it's meant, it'll come to you."

With the others looking on silently, Jack closed his eyes and tried to connect with the rock. Feelings of belonging flooded into him – to the land, the people and its way of life – its very existence.

And then he knew.

Opening his eyes, he pointed at a picture of concentric circles. "That's it," he said.

Albert clapped his hands in delight. "The symbol of the dreaming sites. Reckon you were meant to know."

Jack gave the old aborigine a nod of appreciation. "Thank you for your help."

Ching!

Help appeared. *"OK, OK, OK. I know, I know. You're in trouble again, you can't find your way around, you need me, you can't live without me... What have I gotta do for you primates now?"*

"Nothing." Merle shook her head. "We've managed by ourselves."

There was a momentary silence. *"Excuse me? I thought for a moment there, you said you managed to do something for yourselves,"* Help said disbelievingly. *"That doesn't compute with me. Obviously, I am becoming delusional from overwork and associating with no-brain life forms. I'm gonna have to lie down and take the weight off my processors."* The hologram disappeared into The Server.

"Nice mate you got," observed Albert. A cloud of sand blew into the cave from outside. Albert gave a sniff. "Reckon you'd better be moving on."

Jack nodded, placed his hand against the chosen symbol and pushed. It began to glow. All at once, the cave was filled with sounds of animals, birds and people. The shapes seemed to leap off the wall and spin round and round in a dance of unity. *Like N-Space*, thought Jack. Then there was a flash of light and the companions disappeared.

Albert gave a deep sigh and turned to the cave's entrance to greet the new arrival.

"Where are they?"

"I'm afraid you're too late."

Tingkat gave a growl of annoyance. "Where have they gone?"

Albert held out his hands. "Now, as if I'm going to tell you that." With a shake of his head, the old man vanished into thin air before Tingkat's very angry eyes.

She rushed to the wall. It was covered in incomprehensible patterns. She tried to feel for warmth as Tracer had, but there was nothing. Tingkat stood breathing deeply, considering her next move. "This accursed planet," she whispered. A thought struck her. Tracer had mentioned "another continent". That was it! Which continent hadn't they yet visited? With a snarl she rushed out of the cave.

A mountainside, location unknown

The blinding white of the teleportation vortex gave way to the blinding white of a snowstorm. Wind howled, whipping flakes into stinging flurries. The moment the cold hit him, Jack began to die.

He could make out nothing but the dark outlines of steep mountains. Wind-driven snow snapped at his face and froze. The chill air tore at his lungs, freezing him from the inside out. His thin clothes provided no protection. Desperately, he struggled to walk through the chest-deep snow.

"Merle! Bitz!" he yelled. "Loaf! Googie!"

It was useless; the roar of the storm was all-encompassing.

The snow was piling up into drifts. As the minutes

toiled by with agonizing slowness, and his body froze,
Jack tried to push on seeking the others – shelter – help,
but he could hardly move. The cold was mind-numbing.
Jack felt his senses slipping as the snow piled up around
him. Shivering uncontrollably, his teeth chattering with
cold, he dropped The Server from his frozen fingers and
slumped headlong into white oblivion.

8

Hidden Valley, Tibet

Jack awoke to the sound of birdsong.

He sat up and looked around in amazement. He had slipped into unconsciousness on a freezing snowfield: now he was lying on short, wiry grass beneath a tree covered with pink blossom. Small birds – finches, Jack thought – flitted and squabbled in the branches above, occasionally dislodging petals which tumbled down lazily to join those that had already settled on him.

Jack sat up. How did he come to be here? With a guilty start, he remembered the others. Where were they? Had they been on the mountain, too? And if so, had they survived the freezing cold? He scrambled to his feet and gazed around, frantically seeking some sign of his companions. That was when he realized that he was not alone.

The man who sat under a nearby tree, gazing serenely into the distance, was dressed in simple, homespun robes. On his head was a hat made of straw. He wore nothing on his feet. In his lap he held The Server.

Jack walked towards him on legs that still ached with fatigue. He tried to move slowly so as not to alarm the old man, but his mind was screaming frantic questions, tumbling over each other with their urgency to be heard. Who was the stranger? Why did he have The Server, and would he be willing to give it up? Were the others OK? Were they here? Come to that, where *was* "here" and what was Jack himself doing in this mystifying place?

The man looked up as Jack approached and gave him a tranquil smile. He held out The Server. "This was found beside you. I assume it is of value to you."

Well, at least that answered the first two of his questions. "Yes. Thank you." Jack took The Server with a great sense of relief and turned it over, running his hands over the scuffed casing. It seemed to have suffered no damage, and unless the old man was speaking English (which seemed unlikely) it was still translating. Jack looked into his eyes. "Thank you," he said again. The old man smiled and nodded but said nothing. Jack said, "Are my friends here?"

"They are nearby. The boy, the girl, the ... others. They have not yet awoken."

Jack eyed the speaker with misgivings. How could he know Merle and Loaf were still asleep if he couldn't see them? And why did he call Bitz and Googie "the others"? But he only said, "Where are we?"

The stranger said, "In my valley."

Jack looked up. They were indeed in a valley. A stream ran through green meadows, dotted with wild flowers and groves of trees. None of these were bare of leaves, and many were in blossom. Birds flew and butterflies danced in the still, warm air. And yet on every side towered great, snow-covered mountains. The snowfields and glaciers seemed to end just beyond the furthest trees. The sun shone over the valley, though the peaks surrounding it were shrouded in cloud.

The old man rose unhurriedly to his feet. "Your friends are stirring." Picking up a staff that lay beside him, he made his way unhurriedly down the grassy slope. Wondering, Jack followed.

The stranger was right. Loaf and Merle were stretching and looking around in bewilderment. Bitz was sniffing at the unfamiliar scents. Only Googie still lay peacefully asleep: although, Jack reflected, knowing the cat's habits, she might well have woken up earlier and gone back to sleep from choice.

Seeing Jack, Merle stood up and moved towards him, still staring about her. "I think," she said softly, "this is the most beautiful place I've ever seen."

Jack's guide smiled and bowed to Merle as if she had paid him a compliment.

Bitz sniffed at Googie. "You OK, fleabag?"

Googie cracked an eye open and yawned, stretching and unsheathing her claws. "I was until you came and yelled in my ear, dogbreath." But there was no heat in the insults, and the rival chameleoids sat side-by side as they studied their surroundings.

"What's to eat? I'm hungry!" were Loaf's first words. But his voice was unusually subdued, and he looked around him with an air of appreciation that was at odds with his usual ill-temper.

The old man gave him a placid smile. "If you will come with me, you shall share my food."

"Burgers?" asked Loaf, more in hope than anticipation. "Doughnuts?"

The stranger shook his head. "I am a poor hermit. I have only milk, butter and cheese; honey, fruits and bread."

"Oh, great," muttered Loaf. "New Age slop." But his complaint lacked its usual venom, and he trudged after the others willingly enough.

The hermit's home turned out to be a small, single-roomed dwelling made from white stone with a sloping roof of red sun-dried tiles. There was a rush curtain across the doorway, and rushes on the floor. Inside, a straw pallet served as a bed. There was a low table in the centre of the room, but no chairs; and a brick oven against one wall where (the old man told them) he baked his bread.

The companions and their guide ate their simple meal in silence broken only by the occasional bleating of a small mixed herd of sheep and goats that grazed placidly nearby. They used their bread to scoop soft cheese and honey from the earthenware jars in which they were stored, and drank goats' milk straight from the pitcher.

When even Loaf had declared himself satisfied, they moved outside to sit in the sunshine and gaze out over the valley. After a while, Jack turned to the hermit and said, "Did you bring us here? From the mountain?"

"I?" The old man looked down at his small-framed body, and smiled. "No. That was my companion."

"I thought you lived alone here?" Merle was surprised.

"I do, and I do not." The old man watched a hawk sweeping in lazy circles in the sky above the valley. "My companion is always here, yet he and I have never met."

"That doesn't make sense!" protested Loaf.

"Much is not what it seems," said the hermit quietly. He looked pointedly at Bitz and Googie, who (surprisingly) were managing to lie close together without fighting. "Many are not what they appear to be."

Jack wanted to ask how the stranger knew that Googie and Bitz were not really a cat and a dog, but was wondering how to do it without admitting to their real identities when Loaf broke in. "What is this place anyway?" He waved his arm across the valley. "It should be cold, but it's warm. It's snowing on the mountains, but the sun's shining here. What gives?"

For a moment, it seemed as if the old hermit would

not respond: but at length, he said, "I am one of the last of my kind. We were never many: not since the land of my ancestors disappeared beneath the ice."

Loaf nudged Merle. "Does he mean Atlantis?" Merle shushed him angrily. The old man appeared not to notice the interruption. He went on:

"Once, my people helped yours to build their cities, and gave them the secrets of tools to till their fields. But they turned their cities into fortresses and their tools into weapons, and fought each other until we knew we could not live among them. And so we retreated here, to the high and lonely places of the world, and crafted refuges for ourselves which only we could see."

"Then you must have been here for a long time," Merle said slowly. "Hundreds – maybe thousands of years."

The old man shrugged. "What is time?"

Merle stared at him. "Are you telling us you are not human?"

Once more, their guide ignored the question.

"Will we see your companion?" asked Merle.

The hermit smiled faintly. "Perhaps. He only appears by the light of the moon. At other times, he cannot be seen."

Merle gave the old man a distrustful look. "Are we talking about the supernatural here? Magic?"

The hermit chuckled softly. "Humans! You divide the world into that which can be seen and that which cannot: you measure that which does not matter and give it importance because you can measure it. You divide natural from supernatural: science from magic. Then you worship the one and deny the other." He chuckled again. "So narrow. So foolish." A faraway look crept into his eyes.

"This is crazy talk," Loaf whispered to Jack. "Strange powers – invisible companions – the old guy's been up here for too long. He's totally nutso!"

"He saved us," Jack hissed back. "Or his friend did. At any rate, he's looked after us and given us food, we owe it to him to show some respect." Loaf subsided, muttering.

Jack turned to their host. "I think we have something to do here," he said hesitantly. "We are being followed by dangerous enemies who would destroy your valley in an instant, and think nothing of it, if they thought it would get them what they wanted."

The old man stirred. His face broke into a gentle smile. "As to my valley, do not concern yourself. As to your task – follow me." He stood up in the same unhurried way he did everything, and was about to lead them off when Merle put a hand on his arm.

"Please," she said, "what do you call this valley?"

The old man looked surprised and amused. "I call it nothing. It is simply my valley. But I have heard others name it." He gave the companions an unreadable smile. "I have heard it called Shangri-La."

He turned and set off up the valley, leaving Jack, Merle

and Loaf to recover from their astonishment and scramble hastily in his footsteps.

Tingkat gazed down into the valley with a grim smile of satisfaction.

It had taken her most of the day to find. It was unlikely, she thought, that the inhabitants of this primitive world knew that such a place existed. Even the sophisticated instruments on her stolen ship had scanned this region three times before she had spotted the subtle signs of its presence. Now, she stood on a ledge a few hundred metres above the valley, and watched through the gathering dusk as the humans and their companions followed a slim, robed figure up the valley.

Tingkat lowered her longsight viewer. This time, there would be no low-tech weapons to get in her way: no interfering bounty hunters, no inconvenient so-called gods. This time, she only had to overcome the guardians of The Server and a feeble old man. This time, she would not fail.

Her wrist communicator buzzed. She answered it: and a familiar harsh voice spoke. "Do you have The Server?"

"I will have it," grated Tingkat. "Soon."

"No." The Tyrant's tone did not encourage argument. "I have another task for you."

"But The Server..."

"I have other plans for The Server. Return to your ship.

Await further instructions. Acknowledge."

Tingkat gritted her teeth. "Very well."

She broke the connection. For a moment she stood, undecided. Then she took the communicator from her wrist, and hurled it away from her. It fell for a long time, turning and glinting in the rays of the setting sun.

With cat-like agility, the bounty hunter continued her descent into the hidden valley.

The last of the light was draining from the sky by the time the companions and their guide reached the small shrine that stood on bare rock at the head of the valley.

It was one standing stone, of about shoulder height, with a niche carved in it. Small offerings lay in the niche and on the rocks at its foot. A handful of grains; hair plaited together to make a bracelet; polished stones. The old man indicated the offerings. "Men and women still come up here. Sometimes they leave food, or pieces of cloth. They believe such gifts bring them good luck." He smiled enigmatically. "Perhaps they do." He said nothing more, but indicated the shrine with a wave of his wrinkled hand and stepped back.

Jack nodded. He felt there was a lot to be learned from this apparently defenceless stranger, who had managed to create a small paradise from a terrible wilderness: but they had things to do, and no time to waste. He stepped forwards and opened The Server. "Help."

Their guide showed no sign of surprise or emotion as the hologram materialized above The Server's keyboard. *"Yeah?"* growled Help with its customary lack of charm. But even the cranky hologram sounded less aggressive than usual. It was as if no quarrel could take hold in the little world of the valley.

Wordlessly, Jack pointed at the shrine. Without comment, Help materialized its sunglasses and sent out a beam of ultra-red that washed across the stone revealing only one symbol: a pair of interlocking comma shapes, one white with a black dot, and one black with a white dot, which between them formed a circle.

"Science and magic," said the old man. "Mystery and knowledge. Dark and light." Once again, he gave a faint, enigmatic smile. "Friend and FOE." The companions stared at him: how could this old hermit possibly know about the struggle for control of the whole Galaxy, which was being played out among the stars? But the old man only concluded, "Yin and yang. A circle is only complete when you return to where you began."

Jack nodded, and reached out to touch the glowing symbol.

"Move one muscle more, and you are a dead being."

Tingkat stepped forward from the darkness. She held an energy pistol in one hand. The other was held out for The Server. "No more speeches," said the bounty hunter. "The game ends here. Give me The Server, or die."

As Jack hesitated, the moon rose.

As it emerged from behind the mountains that ringed the valley, a change came over their guide. The stooped old figure grew, and filled out. Its robes fell away, to be replaced by a heavy pelt of snow-white hair. Its gnarled hands became powerful, taloned paws. Its eyes burned. It lifted its arms, threw back its great head, and roared.

Bitz stared at the newly revealed creature open-mouthed. "What do you know! The old guy's a shape-shifter like us."

"Nice transformation," agreed Googie. "Maximum points for style, scariness and technical merit."

Tingkat's mouth dropped open. Even in her adventurous existence, the bounty hunter had never witnessed such a metamorphosis. By the time she had recovered, it was already too late. The bear-like creature, now over three metres tall, moved with incredible speed to smash aside Tingkat's weapon. It roared again – a roar that echoed around the encircling mountains and was answered by the thunder of an unseen avalanche. Tingkat gave a strangled cry of fear, took to her heels, and ran, with the creature in pursuit.

Loaf's mouth looked like a door that someone had forgotten to close. "Did everyone else see what I just saw?" The others nodded, speechless. "What *was* that thing?"

Jack said, "I saw a TV programme once about mystery beasts – you know, the Loch Ness Monster, Bigfoot, things like that. They mentioned a creature that lived in the Himalayas. It was called the abominable snowman. At least, that's what mountaineers called it. The local people called it the yeti."

Loaf's eyes boggled. "That was a yeti?"

Jack shrugged. "Whatever it was, it's given us the chance we need to get out of here." Without hesitation, he reached out for the centre of the yin yang symbol and pushed...

Stonehenge, Salisbury Plain, England

The sun was once more sinking in the West as the companions found themselves standing inside a great circle of standing stones.

"Stonehenge," said Merle.

Jack nodded. "The old man said: 'A circle is only complete when you return to where you began.' There must be one more thing we have to do to complete the Chain."

"Indeed." A hooded figure stepped from behind one of the great sarsen stones. "Such a pity you will not have the chance to do it."

"Yo, dudes and dudettes!" A tattered figure in flamboyant but threadbare clothes stepped from the opposite side of the circle. "Long time no see!"

"Zodiac Hobo!" snarled Bitz.

Googie yowled deep in her throat. "And Tracer!"

9

Merle gave Zodiac a killing look. "I thought you said you didn't work for the FOEs."

Zodiac spread his hands in a gesture of helplessness. "Hey, man, don't get heavy with me. I have to work for somebody."

Jack looked steadily at Tracer. "Why should we hand The Server over to you?" he demanded.

"Because of this." With one of his claws, Tracer pulled out an energy weapon that he had held concealed behind his back. "Of course," he continued in apologetic tones, "it's only a hand weapon – not very big or powerful. But it's more than you have."

"t-mail us out of here, Jack," hissed Merle.

"To where, exactly?" Tracer's elephant ears twitched: Merle realized that she had underestimated the sensitivity of the alien's hearing. "You've already visited all the Ancient Sites on Earth, and activated their defences – thereby, incidentally, ensuring that they will not receive any further incoming teleports. And you dare not teleport yourselves offworld." Tracer gave an unpleasant chuckle. "I believe you have been guilty of what your species figuratively calls, 'painting yourselves into a corner'. Or to put it more crudely, you're out of options." The weapon in Tracer's hand pointed unwaveringly at Merle. He held two more hands out towards Jack. "Give me The Server."

Bitz gave a yap of dismay. "Don't do it, Jack."

"Jack!" yelled Merle. "Don't worry about me!"

"No," said Loaf, eyeing Tracer's pistol nervously. "Worry about how he'll probably shoot me after he's shot her. That's what *I'm* worried about."

Merle waved frantically at Jack. "Get out of here! He thinks if he threatens me, you'll do what he wants."

Jack looked from Merle to Tracer and back again. "The trouble is – " he said, hesitating. "The trouble is, he's right!"

Googie hissed. "You humans are such sentimentalists."

"Jack!" Merle was beside herself with rage. "If you even think about giving this creep The Server because of what he might do to me, I'll never speak to you again!"

Jack shrugged. "If I don't give him The Server, you won't be able to." He placed The Server on one of the fallen stones, and stepped back.

Merle gave a hollow groan. "Jack, I'm not speaking to you – except for speaking to you now to tell you that I'm not speaking to you."

Tracer stepped forward. The energy pistol remained trained on Merle as he stooped and gathered The Server into his arms. "At last," he breathed. "So long in the planning – and now, the endgame begins." With two more of his claws, the elephant-eared being began to tap a complex series of instructions into its keyboard.

Bitz pawed at Jack's leg for attention. "Remember what Janus said? We can't let him try to teleport out of here. Whatever destination he selects, he's going to wind up t-mailing himself right into The Tyrant's rumpus-room with The Server."

Jack nodded grimly. "I know. But there's nothing we can do."

Tracer's expression, as he turned to Jack, was a strange mixture of wry amusement and resignation, mingled with something else – it might almost have been anticipation – even triumph. But, Jack reminded himself, he really wasn't very good at reading alien expressions.

"Kind of you to be concerned," said Tracer softly, "but I am not a complete fool. I know what I'm doing." He looked around at the silent companions: at Jack, who was watching him stony-faced; at Bitz, whose muzzle was drawn back in a snarl; at Googie, whose cat-face was inscrutable; at Loaf, slouching moodily; at Merle, who was regarding him with hatred, tears of frustration welling in her dark eyes. With a return to his old manner, Tracer winked at them. "It's been fun." He held up The Server, and prepared to press the "Send" key...

...just as a shadow fell across the ancient stones. Startled, Tracer looked up.

Zodiac's ship had stolen silently up, and was now

hovering above Stonehenge, almost touching the tops of the mighty stones of the inner circle. As Tracer gaped, a hatch shot open in Trigger's belly. A flexible cargo-handling arm shot out. The hand-like grab at its end swooped with the speed of a striking snake – and pinned Tracer against one of the great standing stones.

Loaf let out a whoop of malicious delight. "How d'ya like them apples, Dumbo? Awesome! Trigger to the rescue!"

Tracer scrabbled furiously at the metallic claw with the three of his hands that were not otherwise occupied. "What is it doing? Has it gone mad? Hobo! Call your ship off!"

Zodiac looked as if he was trying hard not to grin. "Hey man, sorry – like, I must have left it on automatic pilot." He raised his voice. "Trigger! C'mon, baby! Let the dude go, willya?"

"*No!*" Trigger's amplified electronic voice was uncompromising. "*I don't like him. He's not a nice being.*"

Zodiac shrugged. "Y'know, I ain't crazy about the guy myself, but…"

"*He said I was stupid!*" snapped Trigger. "*He called me an idiot machine. He said I was operationally challenged, and he was amazed I could fly. He told me I was clapped out and impotent. He made me fight that snake-thing.*" Trigger gave a shudder. "*And he made me go through that worm hole.*"

"Yeah, yeah." Zodiac waved his arms ineffectually. "But

he owns you, see – I mean, like I don't dig capitalism, but..."

"And he threatened the human Merle," hissed Trigger. *"She was kind to me. She treated me like a person. She gave me my name."* Trigger squeezed the grab tighter. Tracer gave a squeak of dismay and wriggled furiously to get his claw on the "Send" button. Trigger squeezed again. Tracer gasped and dropped his pistol – and The Server.

Merle stepped forward and picked up the gun. "Thank you, Trigger," she said in a voice that fought hard to stay calm. "You can let him go now."

"Awww!" the ship's voice was plaintive. *"Can't I squeeze him some more?"*

"No," said Merle firmly. "We'll deal with him now." Reluctantly, Trigger loosened its grip. The cargo arm snaked back into its bay and the hatch slid closed. But the ship remained on station, humming faintly.

In its shadow, Jack stepped forward. Once more he picked up The Server. He raised his head and faced Tracer, who was rubbing at his bruised chest with all six hands (this was a rather disturbing sight), still gasping for breath.

"There's been a change of plan." Jack tapped slowly at The Server's keys. Tracer eyed him with apprehension.

Merle said, "Do you want me to do that?"

Jack shook his head. "Keep him covered. This is my responsibility. I won't ask anyone else to do it." Tracer's apprehension was clearly turning to alarm.

Jack finished inputting instructions. "The Server is all set." He looked Tracer straight in the visor. "Where would you like to go?"

Tracer's visor flashed erratically. "You're letting me go?"

"Sure. I'm going to t-mail you out of here, like you wanted. There's just one small adjustment to your plan. You're not taking The Server."

"No!" Tracer's voice was almost a shriek. "You don't understand…"

"Arcadia?" asked Jack. "I hear it's very nice at this time of year. Of course, it doesn't really matter where you choose to go…"

Tracer licked his dry lips. In a voice that was no more than a whisper, he said, "Listen to me. Please. You can't send me to the Tyrant without The Server…"

"I daresay he'll be disappointed," admitted Jack. His voice was calm but his expression was as hard as flint. He went on, "I'm only sending you back where you belong. The Tyrant should be pleased with you. You've tried to take The Server from us. You used the MindMelt on Loaf…"

"Yeah!" said Loaf, rubbing his neck and giving Tracer a resentful look.

"You sent the Bug that took Janus into N-Space, and the one that turned Merle's dad into a zombie. You let the Collectors torture Tiresias. You threatened to shoot Merle." Jack gave Tracer a wintry smile. "You can tell the Tyrant that you tried your best. I'm sure you'll be able to explain." His finger jabbed down on the "Send" key.

Tracer's face was a picture of horror and dismay. Even as blue-white light surrounded him and the forces of the tele- portation event disassembled his body molecule from molecule, his despairing cry echoed around the stones of the circle...

"You fool – what have you done?"

And then he was gone.

Jack's shoulders drooped. He sighed.

"Yeah! Great going, Jack! That got the creep off our backs. I hope The Tyrant tears him to pieces!" Loaf gave a jubilant cackle and thumped Jack on the arm.

"Shut up, Loaf," said Jack.

Loaf stared at him. "What'd I say?"

"Like I said," drawled Googie, "humans are sentimen- talists. He's getting a guilt complex because he sent Tracer back to The Tyrant."

Loaf snorted. "Sap."

Merle gazed uneasily through a wide gap at the South- western quadrant of the stone circle. "Guys – I think we'd better move fast."

It was now nearly full dark. The companions gazed around. All around them, bright specks of light were con- verging at speed on the stone circle.

"Bounty hunters," snapped Bitz. "At least fifty of them: t-mailing Tracer out of here must have given them a fix on us. We have to find the last symbol, and activate the

Chain – fast, before they get here."

Jack nodded. "Help."

Help appeared. *"Well, lookie here!"* said the hologram snidely. *"Guess where we are again. You primates can't hardly stay away from this place…"*

"Not now," said Jack. Help subsided, mumbling. "We have one more symbol to find, and we haven't much time to scan the stones."

"We don't need to," said Help smugly. *"I was paying attention when we were last here, even if you weren't. The last symbol is here."* The now familiar purple-red light appeared as a tight beam, which rested on a massive fallen stone. As the companions watched, a strange picture appeared – a glowing serpent, bent into the shape of an O, swallowing its own tail.

The whine of the bounty hunters' approaching craft was building to a scream.

Merle reached out and traced the outline of the snake. "'A circle is only complete when you return to where you began.'" She nodded, as if seeing the solution to a puzzle. "The Ouroboros."

Loaf stuck a finger in his ear, and wiggled it. "Say what?"

"Oo-rob-or-ross," said Merle slowly. She caught Loaf's uncomprehending stare and rolled her eyes. "Later." Hand hovering over the snake image, Merle gave Jack an enquiring look. He nodded.

The bounty hunters closed in. Merle pressed the symbol.

There was a flare of blue-white light from every stone at once, brighter than ever before. The circle of light expanded, racing away to every horizon.

Every time it touched a bounty hunter's ship, the vessel was bathed in light, and vanished as suddenly and completely as a soap bubble. Only Trigger – protected, Jack thought, by its position at the heart of the circle itself – remained.

Then there was silence. The hum of the stones dropped until it was barely audible. Nevertheless, there was a strange air of watchfulness about the ancient circle – as if, at any moment, the quiescent power of the stones could flare up again, to drive away any invader.

Loaf was still staring around in amazement. He turned a bewildered face to Jack and Merle.

"But..." He moistened his lips and began again. "All those bounty hunters ... where did they *go*?"

An unknown planet

A bounty hunter stepped out of its crippled craft, energy weapon at the ready. It gazed apprehensively around at the strange and sinister jungle surrounding it. Horrible noises – shrieks, squawks, roars and snarls – sounded from all sides. Bushes shook.

It spotted a fellow bounty hunter backing away from his own useless vessel. They moved cautiously through the undergrowth until they stood back to back.

"What is this planet?" whispered the first bounty hunter.

"Aaaaaargh!" replied the second bounty hunter.

The first bounty hunter felt an ice-cold chill run down its spine. "Do you mean the planet Aaaaaargh!, with six 'a's, home to the Eyeball-Popping Razor-Toothed Ear-Driller and the most horrifyingly dangerous place in the known Galaxy?"

There was no reply. The second bounty hunter's head landed on the damp earth with a thump, and rolled to a stop at the first's feet.

The first bounty hunter gulped. "I'll take that as a 'yes', then."

Stonehenge, Salisbury Plain, England

"The Ouroboros," said Merle as they stood and watched the symbol fade back into the ancient stone, "is old. Nobody knows quite how old. It occurs all over the world – Egypt, Greece, Iran, you name it. It's the symbol of eternal life – constant renewal. An endless cycle of existence."

Jack nodded. "Like yin and yang."

"And like the O of Outernet," added Bitz.

"Like the ring of a doughnut," said Loaf. In the silence that followed this remark, the others stared at him. Loaf looked uncomfortable. "I'm taking kind of a lateral approach to this analogy…"

"Well, the Outernet as we know it won't last for ever," said Jack. "Not if The Tyrant gets his way. But I guess that's sort of out of our hands, now. The Server should be safe here on

Earth. The Chain is in place. Janus said nobody can break it."

An owl hooted. The air was getting colder. Merle shivered. "We didn't find The Weaver," she said. "But maybe we did enough. Don't you think so?"

Jack shrugged. "I don't know."

Merle moved closer to Jack. "Say – you know what you did back there? When you gave Tracer The Server so he wouldn't shoot me?"

Jack looked at his feet.

"That was…" Merle's voice was husky. "That was…"

Jack waited.

Merle swallowed hard. "That was … really stupid."

Jack gave a shout of laughter. Then he cupped his hands and called up to the ship that was still hovering over the stone circle: "Hey, Trigger! Could you give us a lift?"

Zodiac looked alarmed. "Hey, sorry, dude. Like, I'll be in enough trouble with The Tyrant when Tracer tells him what happened here, without giving you guys a ride. Company policy, man – 'no unauthorized passengers'…"

"*Shut up!*" Trigger's voice snapped out, silencing Zodiac. "*Of course. I'll be happy to give you a ride,*" Trigger went on in gentler tones. "*I'll enjoy having some polite civilized company aboard for once. It will be my pleasure.*"

"Oh, man," groaned Zodiac. "Even my ship gives me a hard time."

Jack turned to the others and said quietly, "Let's go home."

10

Little Slaughter, near Cambridge, England

"Well, dudes and dudette," drawled Zodiac, "It looks like it's the end of the road. Me and Trigger are gonna high-tail it off of this planet once and for all and head for the stars. Like they say: *to infinity!*"

"...and beyond?" suggested Loaf.

Zodiac looked puzzled. "Heck, no. What sort of crazy idea is that? There's nothing beyond infinity!"

The journey from Stonehenge had taken just a few minutes. Trigger had crept in under the air base radar and landed just outside the village of Little Slaughter in order to avoid prying eyes and further missile greetings from the United States Air Force.

The companions stood at the bottom of the ship's landing ramp. Zodiac was at the top, his body outlined by the cabin lights.

"Goodbye, Merle," sniffed Trigger. *"Thank you for my name. I'll miss you."*

Merle gave a nod. "Same here," she said awkwardly.

The ship burst into electronic sobs. Merle shuffled her

feet in embarrassment. She couldn't help feeling that, having only suggested the name "Trigger" as a joke, she didn't really deserve the ship's high regard.

Zodiac gave his battered vessel a pained look. "Oh man, that's all I need, an emotional wreck of a ship!" He jabbed at a button. "Come on, Trigger, pull yourself together." The landing ramp retracted into the ship.

Jack gave Zodiac a final wave. "Thank you for everything you've done."

"In spite of trying not to," muttered Loaf under his breath.

"No problemo, amigos. It's been a blast." Zodiac considered for a second. "Mostly." He considered again. "Well, it's been weird." He gave a theatrical salute. "Plant you now, dig you later."

Loaf frowned. "Say what?"

"I think he's saying goodbye," explained Googie.

"Right on, wild child." The door closed with a quiet *shoosh*.

Trigger's engines coughed into life and within seconds the ship lifted into a night sky that glistened and shimmered with the light of a million stars. Trigger gave a farewell barrel-roll and shot upwards. The companions watched in silence as the ship grew smaller and smaller, before disappearing into the vastness of space.

"Do you think we'll ever see them again?" Merle wondered out loud.

"If we're particularly unlucky," said Googie.

Jack gave a shrug. "Who knows?"

"And who cares?" said Loaf.

"You don't mean that!" Merle's voice was full of rebuke.

"Why not?" replied Loaf. "I'm getting tired of all this saving the Galaxy stuff. It's about time we started showing some concern for *us*. And I'm starting with getting proper food inside my belly – I haven't eaten for hours."

Merle flicked her mobile phone open. "I'll call my dad and see if we can get a ride."

Jack put her hand over the phone mouthpiece. "Merle – if your dad gets hold of me, he'll lock The Server up in the most bomb-proof vault he can find, and hang on to me for questioning for who knows how long. Listen – I'll come to the base and talk to your dad tomorrow, I promise: but right now, I just want to go home and see *my* mum and dad. You lost me somewhere on the trail: you don't know where I am. OK?"

Bitz gave a nod. "Me too. I'm not going back to that pound! There's a Dobermann there I do not want to meet."

Googie arched her back against Merle's legs. "I'd better lie low as well. Now your father knows I can talk, I don't think he'll be quite as relaxed as he used to be about finding me asleep on his confidential files."

Merle nodded. "OK – see you soon." She turned to

Loaf. "I suppose you want a ride?" she said without enthusiasm.

Loaf gave her a hard stare. "Don't knock yourself out."

As Jack, Bitz and Googie faded into the darkness, Merle dialled and held the phone to her ear. "Kirk to *Enterprise* – two to beam up – oh, sorry Dad, just fooling around. Where am I? I'm back. Listen, I know it's pretty late, but could you do me a really *big* favour...?"

USAF Base, Little Slaughter, near Cambridge, England

Merle and Loaf sat at the breakfast bar in Colonel Stone's kitchen. Major Jackson leaned against the refrigerator. Merle's father paced up and down the vinyl flooring, his forehead creased in thought.

On their arrival at the base, Merle and her father had done a lot of hugging and Loaf's father had done a lot of shouting before turning Loaf over to Colonel Stone for a debrief. "Give him the third degree," the Master Sergeant had growled. "Be my guest." But Loaf had refused to say anything until he'd had at least two double-whopper cheeseburgers with fries. These had been ordered from the nearest snack bar. Loaf was currently polishing off burger number two. Merle was picking at a pasta salad and relating, between mouthfuls, the events of the past hours.

As she reached the end of the story, Colonel Stone shook his head. "Incredible." He turned to Major Jackson.

"We keep this to ourselves – for tonight." He gave Merle and Loaf a stern look. "But tomorrow, the formalities start. You say you don't know where your friend Jack is right now?"

"Haven't a clue," said Merle truthfully. After all, he could be anywhere in Little Slaughter at this *precise* moment...

"We'll need to talk to him – and those two aliens. Especially the one who keeps sharpening her claws on my desk. You're going to have to tell the whole story again, and not just to myself and the major here. There are some people from the Pentagon and a 'special agency' heading across the Atlantic to talk to you all."

"Will they be wearing black suits and cool sunglasses?" asked Loaf hopefully.

Colonel Stone raised an eyebrow. "I think that dress code is purely for the movies and television."

"Shame." Loaf seemed disappointed.

Merle's father sighed. "You should have tried to detain this Zobo character for questioning – he could have been real useful in determining threat estimates from Alien Life Forms..."

"But Dad," objected Merle with wide-eyed innocence, "he's a space desperado – a real dangerous type – you wouldn't have wanted us to put ourselves in more danger, would you?"

"I guess not." Colonel Stone frowned. "And no talking

to the press. There's been a lot of interest in the events of the past days."

"Has it made the TV? Are we celebrities?" asked Loaf, hopefully.

Major Jackson shook his head. "There's been a press blackout. All the activity with the hunters was an 'important military exercise'. National Security has been cited. The fuss will die down."

"But what about all the people who saw the Sphinx and the flying snake?" said Loaf. "What are they saying?"

"Apparently the 'special agency' I mentioned have sent agents to track down and talk to the people," continued Major Jackson.

"Are they all having their memories erased with flashy things?" asked Loaf.

"You *do* watch too many movies," replied the Colonel. "I'm not aware that we have that technology. It's more a case of confiscating photos and videos."

"You mean," said Merle incredulously, "the government is trying to explain away something that was seen by thousands of people?"

"It wouldn't be the first time," replied Stone acidly. "It's been put out that there was an accidental introduction of hallucinogens into the Cairo water supply. The authorities in Mexico are telling people some story about weird mushrooms accidentally making their way on to hotel menus. Heck, if we can get away with Roswell, we can get away with anything."

Loaf gave a moan. "So no one is going to know how we saved the Galaxy?"

"We still haven't," said Merle. "The Weaver still doesn't have The Server."

"That isn't your responsibility any more," said Colonel Stone. "It's up to the US government to decide how we should take up the fight with this Tyrant." He rubbed his eyes. "OK. We've all been kinda keeping late hours recently. I guess anything else can wait until tomorrow. The boys from across the pond won't be here until then." He pointed at Merle. "You, get to bed." He pointed at Loaf. "You … just get."

3 The Almshouses, Little Slaughter, near Cambridge, England

"Mum! Dad!" Jack called out. "I'm home!" He pushed through the front door to his house and walked into the lounge. "Mum! Dad!"

There was no reply. Puzzled, Jack wandered into the kitchen. Bitz trotted behind. Googie had elected to prowl around the garden, looking for small furry things to chase. Jack had complained that this was cruel. Googie had said she was tired of being hunted, she thought she owed herself a change of role. Jack had been too tired to argue.

He flung open the door to the sitting room. "Hi! It's me!" Still nothing. Strange – maybe they were in bed –

after all it was late. He ran up the stairs and knocked on his parent's bedroom door. Silence. Hardly daring to breathe, Jack pushed the door open. The room was empty.

Panic flooded through his body. He ran from room to room. No lights, no sound ... nothing.

"Where are they?" Jack's voice cracked.

"Stay calm!" Bitz gave Jack a worried look. "Maybe they went to a restaurant – or a movie..."

"They don't do that!" snapped Jack. "Mum! Dad!"

"Sssh!" growled Bitz. "You want to wake the whole neighbourhood?"

Fighting down his terror, Jack set The Server down on the kitchen table. As he did so, his attention was drawn to what appeared to be a piece of grass lying on the polished wood. Jack wondered how it had got there. He picked it up. His legs turned to rubber and his heart missed a beat. It wasn't grass. It was a strand of hair. Spiky green hair.

Bitz whined. "I hope that isn't what I think it is."

Ching!

Help materialized from The Server. His usual jaunty manner was gone. *"Don't shoot me – I'm just the messenger."* Jack stared at the hologram with dread. *"You've got mail and you ain't gonna like it."* Help disappeared back into The Server.

Jack took a deep breath and clicked on the o-mail icon.

From: **The Tyrant**
Subject: **bait**

Human

I am tired of playing games.

You have something that I want, very badly.

I have something you want – your parents.

You will use t-mail and I will divert you to my headquarters.

You will bring The Server with you.

If you do not, then your parents will suffer.

Do this immediately.

The Tyrant

Jack sat down on a kitchen chair. In his mind's eye, he could see what had happened – Tingkat arriving at the house, subduing his parents (Jack hoped that his father had not struggled) and then teleporting off planet to The Tyrant's lair.

Bitz put a comforting paw on his knee. "Gee, Jack, I'm sorry."

Jack ruffled the dog's ears absent-mindedly. "That settles it, then," he said. "I didn't know where to go next. Now, I do." He ran his fingers over the scuffed case of The Server. "I'm going to get my mum and dad back. I'm going to The Tyrant."

Once you've logged on to the Outernet, use this space to record your identification.

AGENT I.D. NUMBERS

PASSWORDS

Remember to write down your passwords in sequence – and enter your most recent password when you log on.